La Souillonne

DRAMATIC MONOLOGUE

NORMAN BEAUPRÉ

For Greg Chabot who encouraged me
to do a translation of *La Souillonne*

From the same author :

L'Enclume et le couteau, the Life and Work of Adelard Coté, Folk Artist, NMDC, Manchester, N.H., 1982. Reprint by Llumina Press, Coral Springs, FL, 2007.

Le Petit Mangeur de Fleurs, Éd. JCL, Chicoutimi, Québec, 1999.

Lumineau, Éd. JCL, Chicoutimi, Québec, 2002.

Marginal Enemies, Llumina Press, Coral Springs, FL, 2004.

Deux Femmes, Deux RLves, Llumina Press, Coral Springs, FL, 2005.

La Souillonne, Monologue sur scPne, Llumina Press, Coral Springs, FL, 2006.

Before All Dignity Is Lost, Llumina Press, Coral Springs, FL, 2006.

Trails Within: Meditations on the walking trails at the Ghost Ranch in Abiquiu, New Mexico, Llumina Press, Coral Springs, FL, 2007

La Souillonne, deusse, Llumina Press, Coral Springs, FL, 2008.

The Boy With the Blue Cap, Van Gogh in Arles, Llumina Press, Coral Springs, FL, 2008.

Voix Francophones de chez nous----contes et histoires, par Normand Beaupré et autres, Llumina Press, Coral Springs, FL, 2009.

Contents

Preface

I took the character of La Souillonne from my novel "*Le Petit Mangeur de Fleurs*", a *roman-vérité* (a true-to-life novel). Some readers say that it's the most captivating character of this work of autobiographical fiction. I love all of my characters in this novel, which is based on my growing up in a small city in southern Maine, but I'm especially fond of the character of la Souillonne. I'm Franco-American, which means that my maternal and paternal ancestors came from Québec and spoke French. Like most immigrants from Québec at the beginning of the 20th Century, they kept their language and transmitted it as far as the third generation, if not the fourth, in the United-States.

I have to admit that the Souillonne is very dear to my writer's heart. A friend of mine assured me that, after having read the novel, her favorite character was the Souillonne, because it was real and she could easily identify with it. When I told her that the Souillonne was the product of my imagination, my friend did not want to believe me. "But she's real, she's alive, she must have existed," she told me. Yes, the Souillonne is real, but it's a character woven from a non-factual reality. It's a character whose threads were gleaned here and there from my observations and my experiences in life, while I was growing up in my Franco-American neighborhood, where I found the Souillonne. She's the amalgamation of all the Franco-American women that I've met in my lifetime. I realize that she is formed of many parts, some more salient than others, but, in the end, she represents the woman—mother—wife--sister--sister-in-law--aunt--cousin whom I had gotten to know and who had been abused, humiliated, were dejected, stepped upon and marginalized, and who were all contained in this woman, the Souillonne. These women all lived in a society largely organized and controlled by men.

The Souillonne's language is not the international French language. She wasn't lucky enough to exercise her rights to be educated, because the family could not spare her and be deprived of her meager salary. She did not go to school long enough to really get to know vocabulary, grammar and the intricacies of language of the formally educated ones. The Souillonne's language belongs to the people where we, Franco-Americans, grew up. I took the very heart of my inspiration from her, the Souillonne. She doesn't realize that she's the repository and guardian of a glossary and a people. The Souillonne is subjected to name-calling; she's the object of scorn and some people talk about her behind her back. They think she's thick-headed, not too bright, and consider her marginalized. She's sixty-nine years old and she wants to pour out her heart, because she feels a need to do so. The Souillonne is a person with a heart. She has the wisdom of ordinary people whose sharpness of mind renders them somewhat extraordinary. I present her as she truly is without embellishment, without any touch ups. She's sitting in an old rocking chair in the middle of her kitchen; she's rocking herself while telling her stories. They're true stories.

A note on the translation. Writing in the Franco-American dialect was a challenge for me since it's essentially an oral language. I never formally learned how to write it. Sure, there were times I used some words, idioms, and phrases taken from my maternal language in my other works. I have been speaking it since I was a toddler at home in Biddeford as many Franco-Americans did in their own locality. When I went to school, I was told that I had to learn standard French that was taught through books that came from France or French-speaking Canada. Even though our teachers understood our dialect, they insisted on speaking and teaching what everyone called, in our neighborhood, educated French, *Parler bien*, to speak well, which means following all the rules of diction, grammar and writing. At home and in the neighborhood, we did not grow up with language rules, except to learn from our parents, relatives and friends how to communicate in French without worrying about what was considered *bien* [well] by those whose task was to be the watchdogs and purifiers of the French language. So, when I decided to follow in the footsteps of Antonine Maillet and her play,"La Sagouine," -----a monologue in the Acadian dialect-----I was taking a chance of not getting it right. I had to rely, not only on my memory for the literary matter, but on my ear for the sounds linked to specific words in our dialect. I had to reproduce those sounds so that I could be faithful to the dialect that I share with so many other Franco-Americans. Not only the Franco-Americans but the people of Beauce in Canada and other regions in Quebec as well as regions in Nova Scotia with whom we share a common language and heritage. You see, our dialect comes from way back. It's part of our immigrants' baggage, their inheritance and, some would say, their treasure. I believe I met the challenge and succeeded in doing what I had set out to do, write a long monologue in the Franco-American dialect. Now, the dialect does not consist of only dialect words but it's intermixed with standard French words and phraseology, so that it does not sound so foreign to others outside our cultural periphery. In its context, any part of my work is well understood by most people outside of New England. That's why my play, "La Souillonne," was well received and understood in New Brunswick, in Paris, in Talant----a town near Dijon----and Angers in France where the play was performed in October 2008. You see, our dialect is very close to some of the dialects that, to this day, still exist in Normandy, in and around Dijon and elsewhere in France. Of course, French Canadians have little problem with it.

Now, if writing in my dialect was a challenge for me, then translating the play into English was that much more of a challenge, since English, my other language, does not convey well certain French expressions, much less a given French dialect. However, being bilingual, I managed to seek the wording of equivalence for certain expressions that are even difficult to render into standard French, such as *licheux* for *flatteur* (flatterer), *chiendent* for *espèce de graminée* (weeds) and the old term *cavalier* for *prétendant* (boyfriend). I truly believe that I have succeeded in bringing to the reader a version that is close enough to the original. Furthermore, in order to replicate the proximate sounds attached to certain words and spelled differently in our dialect such as, *souère, icitte, moé* and *tèd ben* for the standard French *soir, ici, moi,* and *peut-être,* I worked hard at putting down the phonetic spelling of those words, and the overall results were gratifying to me. But that was in the French version. In the English translation, I opted for a language that approximates the language of ordinary people with their ordinary words. La Souillonne is, after all, a very ordinary person with an extraordinary way about her. I omitted passages that deal strictly with vocabulary words or phrases, since that's nearly impossible to translate well. At the very least, the English translation will allow those who do not understand French to be able to read the monologue and even attend a performance of my play and understand it. So many have shared with me their desire to do just that. Well, here it is. I consider it my best attempt at a bilingual task.

Finally, since this is my play, I've taken the liberty of expanding on certain things here and there. I did not limit myself to a strict translation. That's what happens when inspiration hits you while writing. After I had done the translation, I reviewed the text and tried to make it English, if you know what I mean. I turned my thinking around and stopped thinking in French and started thinking in English. That's when clarifications came and elaborations were introduced in the text as I reworked it. After all, things are said differently in French than in English. Each language has its proper words and expressions and, I might add, its own way of thinking. When all of this is done with skill and correctness, then that's the mark of a truly bilingual person, I might add. I tend to think that, over the years, I have reached a point in my life where I can say that I've attained a very good measure of true French/English bilingualism.

The Guys

I was in love once. I'll never love again. Never on your life. It hurts too much. Well, I'll tell you quite plainly, I love to talk about things and people and, for me, it just has to come out. Falling in love is one of those things. Well, loving turns things upside down. Why do people go gaga over love is beyond me. I don't mean loving your family, your children and your friends. I'm talking about falling in love with a man. Being infatuated and all that. That's what I mean. It's not the same thing. When you love your mother, father, your sisters and especially *mémère* and *pépère* with whom you grew up, well, it's not the same thing. Not at all. There's something natural about it. That kind of love comes out of the family. We're born with it. That's how it works. What can I say? That's the way it is. We're not the ones to set things up, I'll have you know. We think we do, but Holy Malony good St. Anne, we often have the rug pulled from under our feet.

As for me, I can't let myself be infatuated with those guys. Guys who just mill around us women, gawking. They call us creature-gals. I sure have a good mind to tell them that women are not created for their itchy wants. Were all God's creatures but Holy Maloney, we certainly don't belong to men. They think we do, simply because they believe they're much higher in the chain of beings than we women are. Yes, as high as picket fences that tear their behinds, if they try to jump too high. They hang around us and make sneering remarks about us, just to make us feel small. Then on top of it all, the guys always want attention. We're not old rag ladies ready to wipe after them all the time. It's bad enough that my mother wanted us, the girls, to take good care of the boys -----iron their damn white starched shirts, press their pants and scrub the dirt out of their socks before washing them. Oh yes, my dear mother and her boys. Her boys was a serious thing. The boys, the workers and wage earners. We had to guarantee them their best appearance. It was up to us girls to take good care of them. Did she ever sing that tune often to us. From morning 'til night. As if we girls did not do our share of the work. I'll let you know that taking care of the house and the farm is a hell of a lot of work: getting up very early in the morning to take care of the pigs, picking up the eggs, cleaning the barn and taking the cow manure to a tall mound outside, and all that. Oh yes, and at night, we had to milk the cows. That was besides taking care of the farm and the house. In the summertime, there were gardens as far as the eye could see. We crawled on our hands and knees to pull out the weeds and the wild growth until our backs started to hurt like crazy. I saw my father, mother, my grandfather and even my grandmother grinding out an existence on that farm. Good Lord, how they worked hard. I didn't do too much then, because I was too young to work as hard as they did. But I helped out. That was back then in Canada when we lived up there.

Once we got to the States, then it was the house and the mills we had to deal with. Yep, the house chores for women weren't considered work. After all, we were just creature-gals. At that time, I used to tell myself that I would show these lame-brained guys that women are not made out of steel. We can't do everything and, besides, you can step all over us only so long. Tell me about those guys whose brains are stuffed with straw, big lazy men who have a hard time moving their ass around. Oops, sorry for the three-letter word. I couldn't help it. Empty-headed like the straw men out there in the fields. Men, why they can't even take care of themselves. Not even their own brains. I mean the way they think. Empty-headed, that's how. Nothing we can do about it though. That's the way it goes. Men, you want men, well you can have them. The hell with them. Oh, I know, there's some good ones, but they're few and far between.

In the past, the guys used to go and see the girls on Saturday nights. Saturday night was the night to have a party. We didn't have time for that during the week. I mean getting dolled up and being ready for boyfriends. We were much too exhausted to do those things after a hard day's work in the mills. We were wiped out. But Saturday night was the time to shake a leg. My Lord, did I see boy friends. Plenty of them. Some with their faces so shiny because they had scrubbed them hard with strong yellow soap, and others, their faces red as a beet because they were so shy and embarrassed. Still others who pouted because they were left by themselves with no one to bother with them. That's because they couldn't do as they wanted. They always wanted to win; it had to be their way or nothing. As I've already said, there were some who weren't too bad but they were few. Thinly sprouting in the fields, as my father would say. I didn't want to have anything to do with them, those guys who had their hands all over you. Always ready to take advantage of women with their crafty look of a wiseacre rooster. There were also some who looked like bulls. Mad bulls ready to pounce on whoever with their bad mouths. Instead of laughing and having fun, they were as stiff as cardboard and grouchy as bulls. How can you speak to someone like that? I can't get used to those men. Much less having them touch me and far less caress me. Bunch of useless flatterers. How can I get infatuated with someone that disgusts me? I'm sorry, it's not my fault, I'm just made that way.

In the good old days, as the old folks used to say, that's the way things were. But I don't want any of the good old days anymore. They weren't as good as that. Not for me. Wearing yourself out right down to the last thread of energy from morning to night, taking care of a bunch of howling kids and often ruined by bad luck and misery, and on top of that, spending your entire life hoping for a better day, that's not for me. The years gone by are gone once and for all. No, I don't want any part of the good old days. And, let me tell you about tough guys like Peton Lantagne. Oh! he was so big, as huge as one of those big wooden barrels. I mean big. A real tough nut, also. He was always ready to pick a fight with someone. We couldn't even tell him two words and he went flying off the handle. He took everything in with a grudge. Everything mixed up too. He got mad at the least little thing. My God, I remember so well the time we knew him at Sainte-Pirouine in Canada. He used to get into a fight with my father, but he didn't dare lay a hand on him for he knew that my father could face up to him and then lay him flat out on the ground. My father was a really strong man. As strong as an ox, my father was. However, Peton got even in another way. He would leave our house as red as a hot iron, and then he went looking for someone on who to unload his anger. Then he would give that one a real beating. I don't know why. Always contrary to the others, that one. Like an old tomcat that you try to stroke against the rub of the fur. That old tomcat sure takes out his claws in no time and swipes at you. There's always been tough guys like Peton Lantagne. I can't stand them. Well, it's because, all my life, I had to get away from them.

When I used to work in the mills there was Ti Gus Laliberté who always wanted to get into a fight with someone. Even the women. Did he ever make them cry. Not me, I'm not the crying type. I'm thick-skinned. Lord, do I remember Clarinthe Grandmaison. She and Ti Gus used to go at it ever so often. He used to get her goat even though she kept saying that whatever he said would not get to her. She would not get mad at him anymore, she said. Until the next time. It was more than she could handle and she just couldn't get rid of him. He had a way of getting her dander up. Once, I remember very well, he hit her really sore spot. It was about her Sunday hat. Oh, it was a really nice hat, a bluish wine colored hat with an ostrich feather. It really fit her well. She looked so nice with it, walking to church Sunday mornings. She felt swell. A real refined demoiselle, she was. Clarinthe was in style with her beautiful Sunday hat. Even though she wasn't the most beautiful person in the world, she had her good qualities as a person. Good seamstress, good cook and a good talker. She didn't hurt no one. A little too meek and easy-going for me, but she was nice.

One Monday morning, Ti Gus grabs her attention and starts to talk about her Sunday hat. He found it so beautiful and it fitted her so well, he said. She smiled with contentment seeing how Ti Gus was paying attention to her in a nice way. Then came the other side of Ti Gus, the slap-in-the-face side. He started to laugh and laugh out loud. Everyone knew that he was making fun of her, and she didn't catch on. Not only that, but he starts being rude with her and begins by tearing apart her hat with all kinds of ridiculing remarks. He found her hat ugly, that the color resembled vomit, that it had a feather from the ass of a chicken, and he did not stop tearing her and her Sunday hat apart. "You look like a half-baked slut with that damn dime-store hat", he told her. She started sobbing and then she got mad. "You, Ti Gus, you'll never get a woman in your life, darn bully. You're only good at making others angry. You're heartless. How do you want people to like you? You're not even able to talk to anyone with some kindness. Your tongue is always like a sharp knife ready to cut up people. And let me tell you what I think of you. I have a whole lot to tell you. You're not well brought up, you have the tongue in a pig's mouth full of swill, your heart is upside down and you're a half-baked man. They cracked the mold when you came along. A real man knows how to talk to a woman. I don't even know where you come from, certainly not from a woman because no woman could have endured you during nine months. You must come from a bitch.....son of a bitch". She said that without raising her voice. All in a single spurt with a voice that was half trembling, but firm. I would never have believed that she was able to answer him like that. She didn't get mad, she didn't let her nerves get the best of her, she didn't let herself get into a spiteful frenzy. She didn't even cry. But, calling him son-of-a-bitch, that was not Clarinthe. She came from a refined family where not a single swear word was allowed, not even a wrong word against another person. Not even damn. When they got angry, all of the words that came out of their mouths were well measured and well thought out. Softened by the fear of being coarse. Like darn, baloney and Mosus. One has to believe that the time had come for Clarinthe to unload.

A woman can only take so much from men. You can swallow and push back the tears just so much. After a time, we can't take it anymore. It sticks in the throat. Pouring your heart out releases the tension in the brain and makes you less of a rebel because you just want to fight back like a frightened animal who has a tendency to go wild. Enough of swallowing all of the swill that is being thrown at us without saying anything. Enough tears when one is crying like a blubbery Madeleine for whatever reason. Enough of men's disgusting behavior towards us. They have no heart and they take us for little whimpering dogs. We say nothing and we keep on swallowing. Men, bunch of scared creatures afraid to move their carcasses. Too lazy to take care of themselves. They need a woman's hand to spruce them up so that they will not be taken for stupid jerks.

Not that I haven't loved a man. I'm like any other person. I met him many years ago, my Willie. He was not like other men. I mean not like the others who are flattering lover boys, and full of hot air on top of that. Those who think of themselves as being strong and handsome in front of women. All of those guys who have a lot of mouth but little in the noggin. You know, the empty-headed ones. They talk without thinking first. Especially without thinking of others. Big winded braggarts don't think about what women feel deep inside. No, they don't even suspect anything. A man who makes a woman feel as if she's beautiful inside, that one is a real man. I mean beautiful like a flower that opens up to the warmth of the sun. I really think that love is like a sun, full of warmth that goes down to the roots of your hair. I don't know how to say the words that describe love, but I know how it feels.

Well, I met him, the man of my life, a long time ago. It was at a party at the Dumas's who live on the hill. It was wintertime, a Saturday night. I caught him with the corner of my eye entering through the front door of the parlor. He was a bit shy, a bit awkward in his way of presenting himself, but ruddy complexioned, soft spoken and polite in his manners. Yes, I saw him. I saw all of that at a single glance, because my eyes were riveted on him and him alone. Oh, he was rather tall, his black curly hair had beautiful waves in front and his skin shined with cleanliness. Everything about him seemed to satisfy my taste in a man. When Laurette, my cousin, introduced him to me, I looked at his hands and I noticed right away that his fingernails were very clean. His name was William. He wasn't from the neighborhood; he lived about twelve miles next to the woods. I was struck by him as if a bolt of lightning had hit me. Although I was never hit by lightning before-----we say that when something happens so fast that we don't even realize it-----it sure felt like it. I could feel my heart pounding very fast. Like wild. Really crazy. I didn't want it to happen, but when my heart started to beat and beat, I thought the inside of me was going to explode. When Willy shook my hand, I felt as if all of me was going soft like putty. Crazy fool, I told myself. Not me. I wasn't used to feeling like that. I had always told myself that I would never fall in love. Never. That was for other people. Why lose your head over a man? Well, let me tell you that one can fall fast and easy without noticing it. Willy was-----well how am I going to say it-----special. It's not the right word but I don't know any other. No foolish lovey-dovey with him; he said right out what he felt. Everything was straightforward with him. I could feel it inside of me. I think that I started thinking with my heart rather than with my head from the moment I began to be with him. He's the one who encouraged me to do so. Well, by his manners and his thoughts. You see, Willy thought a lot. He always thought before he spoke. Sometimes, I used to get angry inside, because it used to take him such a long time to answer me.

Willy wasn't a man of stupidities. Not my Willy. Yes, I learned to call him my Willy after four or five frequentations. That's how our pastor, *Monsieur le curé*, used to say it, *des fréquentations*. He didn't like it when they happened too often, *Monsieur le curé*. He didn't like two young people being alone together without supervision, but how do you want young people to get to know one another if we don't get together now and then? We never tried to hide ourselves. We always saw one another with the family around us. Oh, I was so proud of him, and I loved my Willy. I loved him a lot. That's what my heart used to tell me. You know, it feels like when everything in you, up to the very tip of your toes, rings out with joy all the time like the church bells ringing. The best word to describe my Willy is "gentle".

He was gentle to the very core and wanted to please me even though I knew that he didn't like what he was doing to please me. Like dancing. He had two left feet and often stumbled. But, I showed him tenderly how to put his two feet in tune with the music. I took him gently without letting my nerves get the best of me. You don't show somebody something if you're an old grouch, you know. In any case, Willy learned how to dance. Not bad either. I also loved to please him. I started to read story books just so we could talk about them. I didn't like stories out of a book, but I started to get used to it and later on, I loved it. I think that Willy would have asked me to marry him if he hadn't had that big crazy accident. My God, even now I have a hard time to talk about it. He worked with huge tubs of boiling water to clean the rust off some pieces of iron. Come to think of it, I don't really know if it was water or some kind of acid. I never saw him do it. But, I know that he worked awfully hard. I realize that everyone worked hard then, but Willy told me once how very hard he worked. His skin used to get drenched with sweat and his eyes filled with it, so that he had a hard time seeing. Lord, it was so terribly hot inside there, enough to melt the light bulbs overhead, he said. Then there were those huge pieces of iron that he had to carry on his back like a large turtle lugging along his shell. When he had his big accident, they told me that he was burned alive. A skeleton of a man. That's all that was left of him, my poor Willy. Oh, how I cried. Cried inside of me after having cried with tears. After that, I told myself never, never would I love another man, not like him. I never did.

This thing with infatuations, I'm not the one who invents all of that, you know. Just go and ask the other women and they'll tell you the same thing, and maybe more. If you're a woman brought up on a farm in Canada, then you'll accept the fact that we women were very docile, just like *Monsieur le curé* wanted us to. We bent over backward and we shut up. Once we got to the States, we learned a thing or two about living, and how to fend for ourselves. First of all, we worked in the mills and we got paid. A pay check! How that did your heart some good. Back on the farm, we worked from morning 'til night and we didn't even get a single penny for our work. We were expected to work for nothing, because everything was in common. We all had to struggle together and get by. But in the States, for most women, we realized that we could do any trade and run all of that machinery given the chance, and if we put our mind to it. We weren't as stupid as they thought us to be. A salary. Wow! That really did the heart some good.

The Mills

Let's talk about the mills. The damn mills. Well, they weren't so bad after all, but they often got you mad. Mad as an enraged cow. That's how we say it in French, *d'la vache enragée*. We often were that mad. Did we ever take in some bullshit in those mills. Sometimes the warp would break for the weavers, the threads snapped for the spinners, you know those who worked with bobbins, and even the rovin' didn't go that well, some of the time. And as for the bosses, well let's talk about them for a minute. There were some who were good, some not so good, and then the bad ones. Shit house bosses who always had bullying sounds stuck in their throats, and who didn't know how to talk to people. Real blow hards. Mad as hell, most of the time. Most of them were Yankees or Irish who knew how to lick the behinds of the big bosses upstairs. All of them with English names-----misters. There were also some French-Canadian little bosses-----second-hands, they were called-----but those there, we could at least talk to them in our own language and give them a piece of our mind. On the other hand, there were some who treated us well. Some even learned French, and we got along just great. All of the bosses were men, never women. Women would have been too jealous to boss others. They were not all like that, but most of them were. I think it's because we had been pushed aside for too long. That's my way of thinking. After all, we were creature-gals. The pastors had pushed us aside, our fathers had pushed us aside, our brothers had pushed us aside, our uncles, our cousins and all the men who had learned to push women aside. Aside from their big fat-head feelings and the highfalutin place they had given themselves in society, since the beginning of creation. It was their own way of claiming things, because I don't believe that God made them better and brighter that us women. It's so very true that Eve was created out of Adam's side, but that doesn't mean that God wanted the men to push women aside.

Yes 'mam, did I ever work hard in those mills. Hard as hell. In the summertime, sweat pissed out of our backs right through our bras down to our shoes. Soaking wet. And there was no stopping, no siree, you couldn't let the breaking of a single thread happen, nor let the looms slow down any. Weavers for life. That was us. Oh, how we struggled to earn a living in a very large room full of cotton dust that entered your nose, went down your throat and even blinded you, so much lint was there in the air. On top of it all, the humidity that was sprinkled over your head was so bad that it sapped all of our strength. Everything stuck everywhere even down to our underpants where your bums stuck together like big wads of wet cotton. Talk about hard times at old mill pot. The pot was a damn big one. A huge pissing pot full of piss and vinegar. We were stuck in there for life, at least for our working lives, or until you couldn't move a finger anymore. Dead petered out. Some lasted for years and years in those mills. Some for forty, forty-five and even fifty years. They worked as hard as the shuttle constantly hitting the frame. Pam-pam-pam-pam! Enough to make you go nuts. But, I loved working, damn crazy fool that I was. It gave me the drive to show those people who bossed us around that I could do nice work, and that women, like me, knew how to work. I was so proud of our good Canadian women. *Nos bonnes Canayennes.* They worked hard without complaining. It's true that, from time to time, we gave our bosses a hard time because they didn't understand why there was rotten work, now and then. That's because they gave us shit to work with. You can't do nice work with something cheap. We women, we know quality. We want to do quality work because we're proud of what we do. We don't do bad work on purpose. We weren't brought up that way. Rosée Deschambeault was a terrific weaver. She would make those looms run like a top, humming along without a breakage. She was always nice to everybody, even the big bosses and the supers. We didn't bother much with those fat heads. Always with a smirk on their faces. They didn't even know we existed. Oh, they could see that we were there running their looms but, we, the weavers and the battery hands, we didn't count for nothing. Bottom-of-the-rung people, that's all. Besides that, we were women. They probably thought we had no feelings to speak of, since we came from the farms up in Canada. They couldn't even call us by our names, as if we were zeros. They didn't want our heads nor our hearts. What we felt inside, no, all they wanted were our hands. Mill hands, we were. Real cold-faced jerks. Did they think that we were empty-headed and that we were stupid because some of us only went to school for only a few years and couldn't do too much with that? I would have liked to tell them that we women were intelligent. Not schooling intelligence, but life intelligence. We knew how to live, how to do things as they should be done. We could certainly manage to get out of any hole. We knew how to work and get things done. No, our big bosses only noticed men's work, especially if they were loom fixers. It's because loom fixers often saved their butts over and over again. Without them, looms would not have run, and besides, some of these looms were as old as the hills. It was junk. But some loom fixers managed to do something with nothing. They knew how to make those looms work, I tell you. There was a lot of genius-thinking in those guys. Canadians were not all stupid, I'll have you know. Very good workers. The big bosses knew that too well, and they would go up to them and flatter them with nice words. Never with a bit more money, though. As soon as one of our workers started mentioning a raise, oops, the bosses left in a hurry like scared rabbits. Scared and greedy at the same time.

It's true that sometimes one of the bosses eyed a girl who looked nice. Always looking to snatch one with his staring eyes. And there were some who talked nice to some of the girls, only to have them fall for these big asses while taking advantage of them later on, but that's another story. As for me, I was never bothered, for the simple reason that I wasn't pretty, a bit awkward with big haunches, a belly that stuck out like that, because I didn't wear a corset----the reason being that I couldn't get used to one. I never looked at them with goofy eyes, as did some of the girls. So they never bothered me with that lovey-dovey foolishness.

Infatuations in the Mills

Before I start on infatuations in the mills, I'm going to tell you what I think about all of that. It's not worth it. It's simply not worth it. At all. When you love someone you love with love, not with infatuations that come and twist the heart and sometimes break it. All too often it turns into lies. Then, it's always the woman who's to blame and who suffers for it. The guy, well, he always manages to come out of it clean without too much difficulty. Infatuations last a few brief moments for him, and he can easily get rid of them like an eyelash stuck in the eye. No more than that. But the woman, yes, the poor woman. I've seen some who had their hearts broken because they believed these guys. Son of a beeee. I can't say that word. Sounds too gross. Did they think that these guys were going to leave everything behind just for them? They had what they wanted. All they wanted was to have their fun with a girl and satisfy their appetites of the flesh. Appetites of the flesh seem to delicate for me. I would call that fire up the aaa--aas--behinds, I mean to say. Why do men keep their feelings in their pants while women keep theirs in the heart? I knew one woman, Madeleine-----I won't say her real name because she was a really good person who suffered a lot in her lifetime, and besides, her children are still living. Let's say it this way, she landed in hot soup. Or I should say in shit-----excuse the word. Besides, he was a married man. He wasn't a bad guy, very pleasant and even likeable, but he should have kept his place as a married man. In any case, Madeleine got infatuated with him. She used to talk to me about him because she trusted me. I told her and

I told her, be careful Madeleine something bad is going to come out of this, if you let yourself be carried away like that. You're the one who's going to suffer. But it was bigger and stronger than she could bear. She couldn't help herself, she told me. She loved that man like mad. He could have done anything with her, so strong was the pull. Oh, yes the infatuations of young people. Madeleine was only eighteen years old. He must have been ten, fifteen years older than her. Anyways, it happened. She got pregnant. She had a way of hiding her bulge especially from her family. Well, with time she delivered a baby boy. When she presented herself and the baby to her father, he told her flat out, "If you want to stay here, you have to get rid of that bastard." What will people say and think? That's all that he thought of. He didn't think about his daughter a single minute. He only thought of himself. Well, there you have it, that's a man for you. Madeleine didn't know where to turn. She had no money, no home. She wound up by giving her child away. She gave it to her sister who couldn't have any. It must have broken her heart. Giving her child away. My God, she never told her child about it even when he was older. He always believed that she was his aunt. Her sister and her husband never told him either. He grew up and later got married, never knowing who his real mother was. The two who adopted him worked real hard in the mills to make sure that their adopted son would never set foot in the mills. And to the very end until their death, they never revealed to him who was the real mother. It's much later while Madeleine was dying of cancer that she opened up and told her child that she was his real mother, and that she wanted to die with a clean heart. What a weight lifted from a child's shoulders to get to know the truth at last. The truth was, he was the son of an unmarried mother who was rejected by his grandfather as a bastard. Not that he wanted to hear that he was a bastard, but, finally, he knew the real truth. He accepted it like someone who finds his identity in life, and Madeleine died with a clean heart, relieved. No more remorse. She no longer felt guilty about abandoning her own child. After all, she had been forced to do it. It's not what she wanted to do, but what her father wanted her to do. All mixed up on account of a man who should have known better and by a father who had stopped her from doing what she had wanted to do. Her very own father. What a fix. Yes, infatuations demand a heavy price. Imagine letting yourself be handled like putty in the hands of married man. It doesn't make sense. I know that things are not easy and not always too clear, and detaching yourself is hard, but you have to use your head sometimes or else things will go wrong. That's why I always was leery of those infatuations.

Now let's talk about old maids. I don't mean those who don't get married, who work hard, who do their duty at home and mind their own business. No. I want to talk about the old maids that look mad all the time. You know, those who always have a frown on their faces and who walk with a tight ass----sorry for the a-word again. Some old maids have known love, but the real old maids were never touched by it. Didn't even know what loving a person was. Not even a mother, a father, sister, brother or relatives. No one, I tell you. You know what I mean. There are some people who live an empty life, empty of love. Maybe they feel some kind of love inside, but they never show it. Not even to those who are close to them. And, I'm sure it hurts. They live like creatures made of wood. Hard wood almost like stone. No feeling, no sunny smile. You'd think they were angry all the time. We don't dare look at them straight in the eye because those persons there would tear up your heart. Not only the heart but also the noggin. We don't know what to think with people like that. No affection at all. It must be a miserable life. And those old maids who come out of those families without love, they stay angry and frustrated all life long. It's a good thing that they're not married because they could pass on their rage to their children, if they ever got married. Can you see a man married to such a creature? She'd try to straighten him out her way and he'd become a spinster-man. Two mad hens living together. Well, I mean a rooster and a hen, mad at each other. Think about it.

I knew an old maid who got married at forty-six to a widower who had five children. He so wanted a mother for his children that he ran after the old maid until she agreed to marry him. Cyprien Lamontagne was his name. People called him Ti Croc. He promised all sorts of things to the old gal. But, what had won her over was the fact that Ti Croc promised her that she'd be the boss over everything in the household. Even the money. Well, she started controlling everything: the children, the household, the money and, of course, the husband. They were all scared of her. Everything worked by fear in that household. They were all afraid of going against her say-so. Ti Croc was so afraid of her that he used to hide inside the house so as not to face her. As for the children, well, they were old enough to handle the situation and avoided her entirely. There was one young girl who got married just so she wouldn't have to stay in that house. Ti Croc had thought all along that the old girl would change once married but, My Lord, she got worse. The two of them didn't even sleep in the same bed. Everyone knew about that. Well, because people started talking about it. Poor Ti Croc.

One day, Delphine, her name was Delphine-----I didn't want to tell you her name because I didn't want to start rumors, but it's out now-----she found her little husband dead. People called him her little husband because Ti Croc was only four feet eight inches tall and the old girl measured almost six feet. She buried her little husband and she wore mourning clothes for an entire year. No one found any difference because Delphine always wore black. Black dresses, black hats, a black coat, black stockings and black shoes. She probably wore black underpants too, but no one knew about that-----they probably didn't make black underpants then either. In any case, the children left, one after another. She found herself alone once more. She had no one, absolutely no one. She started taking in stray cats. Some were mangy, some dirty, some as skinny as a rail, and others half lame. She learned how to take care of them. For once in her life, she could, at last, offer a bit of love to someone or, in this case, to an animal. I think that became her salvation, poor Delphine. Sometimes people would catch her smiling, not too often, but from time to time, she did open up a bit. We even stopped calling her the bitchy old maid. People began calling her the cat lady. It's not at all funny when one becomes a mad old maid, only because of a lack of love while growing up. And you out there, you know that there are nuns, those holy ones there, who turned out as old maids, not to mention the old bachelors.

Drinking and Boozing

I really didn't want to talk about drinking and boozing, but I just can't help myself. I have to admit that all of that drinking stuff is part of our culture, we French-Canadians. I don't mean culture with a capital "C": style, beautiful homes, dishes that match the butter dish and the sugar bowl, and all that. No, I mean culture with a small "c" for people like me. Not that people of high culture didn't drink, but they did it with their noses up in the air. We, the small people, drank with our own. I'm talking about the men who drank, because women feared the damn liquor terribly. When you get right down to it, women were afraid that their husbands would spend all of their pay on booze Friday night when they got paid. That's why they hated booze so much. The women belonged to the "Carcle Jeanne Arc", you know, the Joan of Arc Circle, and they wanted so desperately for their husbands to belong to the "Carcle Lacordaire", the men's part of the organization who wore the blue button. It was a bunch of non-drinkers who wanted everybody to lay off drinking. As for me, I never liked to join those people, for the simple reason, they were hypocrites. There were some who wanted to convert others and then there were some who wore the blue button and who drank like a fish in hiding. Do you think that the Lord never drank in his life on earth? The marriage at Cana, just to name a place, that's where he turned water into wine and everyone drank, even the Blessed Virgin, I'll have you know. They were part of the people, the Holy Mother and her Son. They didn't hide it, I mean their drinking. And then, those apostles, they all drank wine at the Last Supper. The gospels don't hide that.

I'm not too too Catholic like many are, and I didn't spend too much time in school, but I've learned a thing or two, enough to know these things. Some people call me a loose-grain Catholic, but I prefer being loose-grain than being tight-grain kisser of altar rails. Those that like to show off and pretend they're smarter and holier than others. Not me. I am what I am.

Let's talk about booze. Back home there was, among many kinds of liquor, the *caribou.* It was a mixture of wine and alcohol, then the *bière ferrée,* beer in which they dunked a hot iron to give it a snap; the *petit blanc* homemade pure alcohol. That one gave you a good kick in the stomach and in the legs. Then there were others. I don't know them all. I'm not a drunkard. The *bagosse* came from up Maine where the Acadians live. I met some who went on a God Almighty binge. Always between two winds, as we say in French. Why, they could hardly move their backside, so drunk were they. Seven days a week, from Monday to Sunday. I'm surprised they went to work just the same with a sloshed head like that. But they managed to do their jobs. How they smelled. Not washed, not cleaned up at all for weeks on end. Poor them, the Lord's creatures who had become slaves to booze----the devil's slaves, I'd call them. Our French language has all kinds of words to describe drinking and boozing, but I'm not going to bore you with them. Damn booze. Pardon my words but that's the way I see it. And, I'm not the only one who sees it that way.

My father was a drunk. He gave my mother a hard time with his drinking. Poor 'ma, how many times she picked up after him. Time and time again. Sometimes she would find him out in the streets half drunk. She would drag him home all by herself. My mother was a strong woman. But poor her, once home, papa continued to drink until his eyes became glassy like a mirror and burned out like a used electric bulb. She used to say that it was better seeing him drink at home rather than outside during the winter months. She didn't care any longer about what the neighbors thought and said, because everyone knew about papa. People had stopped, a long time ago, making remarks about his condition. On account of my mother, because they pitied her. Probably also because of the children. I was young then and it made us children sick at heart. Even today, sometimes tears are so close, I could just cry. Ti Marbre, they called my father. His real name was Aimable. Aimable Hormidas Sansoucis. What a strange and funny name, but that was my father's name. I loved my father. My mother's name was Ernestine. My father called her Crépisse. I don't know why. I'm sure it was some kind of term of endearment. My father never beat up my mother. Never. I never saw him even touch her either. Never touched the children either. He was a mild man, my father, not too much talk in him, but mild like a milking cow that let's herself be milked without moving at all. Not even her tail. I guess you have to believe that my mother had found something good in my father for her to marry him. True that she told Maybelle, her best friend, that she knew her Ti Marbre drank, but that she would change him once they were married. Change him? Good Lord! Women loved to say that. They thought that, somehow, marriage would change things around. When people have that in their blood, like papa did, there's nothing that will change that. Yes, I know there are always promises made, but that's what's called drunken promises, *des promesses d'ivrogne*, as we say in French. Promises full of holes like a sieve. I know because it's the same thing with my Médée. But I'll talk about that later.

Now, I'm going to tell you a little story about drunks. Not to speak bad about my uncle, but because it shows how people, especially women, go to great lengths to fight booze. Also, how we don't like others to know our business, especially when it comes to drinking. Well, my uncle Edouard-----we called him Tapis and I don't know why-----he always had a taste for booze and fun. The taste for woman too. Women found him very attractive with his handsome face and his wavy auburn hair. And he was nice with everybody, a nice personality. He loved parties. He spent money like water running through his fingers. He bought rounds of drinks for everybody. He was President of the Raquetteurs, the snowshoe club. Everyone loved Tapis.

One day, my aunt, Albina, told my mother that one of her brothers-----the one that she liked best-----had told her that if he ever caught my uncle drunk in town or anywhere out on the streets, he would stop talking to him. My mother was my aunt Albina's best friend. They used to tell everything to one another, and I mean everything. Things they would not repeat to others. Well, I guess that my uncle heard what his brother-in-law had said about him from somebody else, and he told his wife about it. My aunt got really mad with my mother thinking that she was the one who had spilled the beans. One Saturday morning-----I will always remember that day-----my aunt Albina came to our house mad as hell, and she began to shout all kinds of things at my mother. How she felt betrayed, how she could never trust my mother again, and how mad she was. So mad that she started to scream at my mother, "You damn slut!" *Ma vache!* in French, but how do you translate that? My cow? It doesn't make sense. See what I mean by translating certain things in English. I was afraid of my aunt when she did things like that. I loved my aunt. After all, she was my godmother. A godchild can't hate her godmother. But, at that very moment, I started not to like her. I wanted to get away as far as I could from all that quarreling. That word "slut" had struck me right in the gut. Straight to where it hurts deep down. Poor aunt Bina, she wanted so much to protect her brother Harvey. He had changed his name from Hervé to Harvey. He probably wanted to be like the English. He liked to be big and show off, Harvey did. Anyways, you have to believe that she loved both husband and brother so much that she didn't know where to turn, and it all came out in front of my mother. Black rage, I call it. My poor mother just couldn't defend herself because she couldn't move or say anything. Words would not come out of her mouth. All of that for damn booze. Even my aunt drank a little now and then. She did it because she wanted to have some fun and join her husband, and she did it very quietly. Otherwise, she would have been all alone in her little corner.

My mother never drank. She didn't like it. Good Lord, can you see mother taking a drink in a bar room or even going into a liquor store. Not that she was a *Jeanne d'Arc*. She never wore the blue button. She had seen too much. She had endured too much, especially with my father. Yes, you have to believe that we French-Canadians have that in our blood, especially the men. It probably comes from the Indians and the *coureurs de bois*----those runners of the woods----with all of the mixed blood. My grandfather used to tell me long stories about the *coureurs de bois* of the olden days. I don't know too much about history, our ancestors and all that. I never went to school long enough to get to know these things. All I can say is that I heard about it. That's all. There must be a lot of mixed blood in our family. The taste for booze flows in our veins and it makes the men wild at times. I have to admit that with time and the hard times in my life, I learned to take my little drink too. It soothes me at times. It soothes me when I know that others call me the Souillonne. Yes, the Souillonne because with the years gone by, I started to neglect myself. I no longer had the taste for nothing. I gained weight and I was up to two hundred pounds. Lordy-lord! My behind was very big, my stomach was out there like that, and my boobs hung down to my belly. I looked like a Souillonne. Some thought that people called me the Souillonne because I never washed myself. That's a damn lie. I always took care to wash myself. I probably looked sloppy, but I really wasn't unclean. It's because I stopped ironing my dresses and I wore my stockings rolled up around my ankles and my hair wasn't curled. I didn't care. As long as Médée did not leave me for another. He didn't mess with me and I didn't bother him. I know that some think that Médée and me are living together without being married. You know, shacking up. We don't sleep together. I love my Willy too much to shack up with another man. I just live with Médée for company. Médée likes to drink. Not that he's a drunkard. No. He likes to have his little glass of beer and he makes it last a long time. One bottle of Ballantine Ale per day. One big green bottle from Audie's market. That's all. But people believe that we both drink together all day long. They can believe what they want, I don't care. Let them call me the Souillonne. That doesn't bother me at all. What hurts me are the insults the kids throw at me in the back yard. Nasty things about my appearance, my awkward ways and my dumb head, so they shout: Fat-ass lady, sloppy woman, that I don't wear underpants because I'm touched in the head, blah, blah, blah. Things like that. But I'm not dumb and I'm not that fat and ugly. It hurts me just to think about them mocking me without really knowing me. They hear it from the grown-ups, those sharp tongues who tear me apart without knowing what it's doing to me. I don't have a hard heart. I would never do that to them. Not a one. I'm not made of stone, I feel inside my heart like others do. I think that all of that bad mouthing started with *Monsieur le curé* one Sunday morning.

I was at high mass. I washed myself real good with a new bar of scented soap that Laura Dupuis had given me for my birthday, and it smelled good. It made my skin soft and clean. I ordinarily use a regular bar of soap but that morning, I wanted to look and smell pretty. Not that I was *orgueuilleuse*----filled with pride----no, but I wanted to present myself before the Lord feeling special. After all, going to high mass on Sundays was special. At least for me. So many women put on their finest for Sunday mornings and I felt I could do the same. After all, I wasn't so very different from the others. I have feelings just like other women, I'll have you know. Then I put on my best dress and my beautiful hat. The one with the red feather and the purplish ribbon. I thought I looked swell and I felt pretty. Why, even Médée noticed me and told me I looked swell. Well, that morning, the *curé* began to talk about those who are the cause of scandal in the parish. Like those who go to beer joints and who show bad behavior. Bad example, he said. Especially for the young. And he started to wave his arms above his head, and he had fire in his eyes. He didn't stop looking in my direction. He was really at it. All of a sudden he started to stare at me straight in the eyes. Staring and staring as if I was the guilty one. He didn't point a finger at me, but he came close to it. I began to get red in the face. I felt shame creeping up on me. My face turned as red as a beet. I felt so ill at ease. Yet, I hadn't done anything to be ashamed of. I didn't know what direction to turn to. Everyone seemed somewhat uncomfortable for me. There were some who started to cough and look at me sideways. I really felt embarrassed, even if I hadn't committed any scandal. Just the fact of seeing *Monsieur le curé* get angry with people like me who appeared and acted differently than others, was enough to turn people against me. I was sure. Yet, I had done nothing to deserve *Monsieur le curé*'s rage. He made me feel as if I wanted to go and squeeze myself into the hole of a mouse, so ugly did I start to feel at that very moment. I don't know what got into me, but I stood up, I looked at the *curé* straight in the eye, I climbed over the legs of the people sitting in my pew, and I got the hell out of there. And I went out through the front door, the tall ones. I didn't want people to think that I was ashamed. I wasn't ashamed at all. I had done nothing wrong. I had not hurt anybody. I'm not the one who was the cause of scandal in the parish. It was the *curé* who had scandalized me. Isn't it strange how some *curés* act sometimes. Like demons, not like priests. I guess that *Monsieur le curé* had not read his gospels as they should be read. Myself, I don't know too much about the gospels, but I do know enough to understand that Christ speaks to us of not judging others without knowing them. That, I know. I never set foot in church again after that. Why should I? To have him say that I scandalize others? Especially the children? I love children. I would never hurt them. Not on my life. I'm not made like that. I am who I am. That's all.

Who I Am

Well, it's time that I tell you who I am. I've talked about everyone else, but I haven't talked about me. I want to tell you who I really am. Not that I like to talk about myself too much, but I'm a person too. I have feelings and I'm not dumb. I have a head on my shoulders, I'll have you know. I'm made the way I'm made, and I say that with an open heart. I don't like to tell tales and cover things up. I'm going to tell you the truth about myself. I'm Maybelle Sansoucis. My mother named me after her chum, Maybelle Sarasin. I grew up with that name. Not that I didn't like my name, but there were some, especially the guys, who just loved to yell at me, "Maybe pretty, maybe *belle*, grassy Maybelle." Not pretty like the flowers not even the dandelions, you know, the piss-in-the-beds. They wanted to tell me that I was pretty like the grass that grows. Sometimes nice, sometimes ugly. That's why we walk on grass; we step all over it. I didn't pay any attention to them. Real crackpots. Then I used to tell them "Go fly a kite, you snotty kids". Today I'd tell them straight out, "You bastards!"

As for the name, Souillonne, that some people call me, well, it comes from the neighborhood where I live. I've lived here fifty-nine years in the same parish and on the same street. I was born in Canada. We moved here when I was six years old. I was the youngest in the family. We came to the States because things weren't going so well on the farm. There were many in our village who were starving. No, it definitely wasn't working out for the people on those farms over there. Did my grandfather cry when we left for the States. He went to live with one of his boys, my uncle Eugène. I never got to know him too much. After that, we found this rent on the second floor. It wasn't too far from the mills. With time, my father was able to buy the house from the old Greek, a man called Mr.Throumolos. It will always be my mother's and father's house. They earned it, I'll have you know. My father and my mother worked like dogs to finally earn the right to buy a house. I'll never sell it, no siree. After my father died-----and I have to tell you he died a drunk-----I stayed in the house with my mother for twenty-three years. I lost my brothers and my sister when they were still young. My brothers moved away and my sister, well, she died here at home. I worked in the mill to help support my mother. She didn't have any money, my poor mother, not a penny left after she had buried my father. Good thing that the house was paid for. She shelled out a lot of money to bury him the way she wanted. No insurance, since my father didn't believe in that. She wanted so much to give him a proper burial, because she loved my father in spite of his drunken binges. And, she didn't want to hear others say that she had neglected her husband. "People won't say that I sent him off poorly," she told me. She used to tell me that over and over again. Maman was made that way. What can I say. Poor papa, he didn't go as a poor man, he went off in a beautiful black carriage with all the trappings.

I'm not one to show off. I take things in life as they come. Sometimes things come hard and fast, not like I would want them to, but we can't turn things around. Things are all prearranged for us creatures of God that we are. Like it or not, that's how things are. We can crab about things, we can get angry and we can just rebel, but it won't change a darn thing. But as for me, I'm going to tell you, I take things as they come. We mustn't let things get the best of us. If you're born for little things in life you're going to stay like that no matter what. That's what Mrs. Atkinson used to say. She's such a lovely lady, Mrs. Atkinson. She always minds her own business. She always has a good word for me. There are those who don't like her because she's a Yankee, but not me----Yankees are those who are not Irish and speak good English. I really like her. We somehow learned how to understand one another half French, half English. Some say that with time we're going to lose our French language if we continue to speak English. So, what do you want? We live in a country away from Canada and people speak English everywhere over here. It's true that almost everyone I know speaks French, but more and more do we find that young people learn and speak English. I have no problem with that. It's nice to be able to use two languages, though. You have to know how to sort things out in life. We're going to lose our French only if we want to lose it. No one is going to take it away from us. That's what I think about it and that's the way I am.

I'm going to tell you a little story. I had a cat once and I had her for a very long time. Her name was *Minoune*. I guess we French-Canadians can't find names for our tom cats and our female cats, so we call them *minou* and *minoune*. Yet, we find names for our dogs, our parrots, our horses and even our pigs. My aunt had a dog that she named Blackie. Of course, the dog was black. She could have called him *Ti Nouère* but that was her business. Her brother, my uncle Ludger, who lived in Rhode Island, named his horse, la Chestnut. It would have been odd for us Francos to call the horse by the real French name of *Châtaigne*. It's a word that's too Frenchy French for us. As for his favorite pig, really a sow, he called her *la Verrâsse*. A way of showing his affection for her. Coming back to my story, my cat did not like tom cats. She looked at them with her mean eyes every time she met one. The tom cats prowled and prowled around her and really wanted to get her. But, she didn't want any part of them. One day, a big yellow tom cat, real dirty and full of scabs, started to run after her. She scratched him in the face and bit him on one ear. The tom cat let out such a long loud screech that the entire neighborhood heard it. He couldn't help himself. A real deadly yell. She had defended herself like a cat knows how. It's because she didn't want any part of tom cats, especially the mangy, dirty ones. Sometimes I see men exactly like that. Dirty and mangy. Prowlers too. Me too, I wouldn't have liked to have an old tom cat jump on my back just to satisfy his coon cat's itching. I'm probably not the best person on earth, but that's the way I am.

Don't go thinking that I'm afraid of men all the time, There are some who disgust me while others leave me indifferent. On the other hand, there are some I could love with time, if I would let myself go. But, there aren't too many of them. It's because I've seen too many things in my life, too many slaps in the face, too many blows with the fist, too many times making a woman cry, too much bad blood, too much drunkenness, too much swearing and hollering and too many disgusting things. Worse, too often came the hurt of the hollow silence of abandonment. A-b-a-n-d-o-n-m-e-n-t. My God! All of that stays stuck in the throat and in the heart for so long.

That's me, I'm made that way. I'm made up of rags because I have years of rags in the blood. Rags for polishing, old rags to wear, rags to braid carpets, torn rags in the heart because it's been broken too many times. I'm made up of old rags to mop up things, because I've washed many floors and stairs in my life; rags for cleaning toilets because did I ever wash toilet bowls and mop up after people in my life. I suppose that you could very well call me the old fat rag lady. I'm made up of soap because I'm not the dirty messy lady, the *souillonne*, that people think I am; I like to be clean. With soap and water, we can wash and scrub; with soap in the soul we can clean the heart out. I'm made up of good warm bread. Did I ever bake bread in my life. Three big batches every week like my mother showed me. We were only three in the house after my brothers left and then my sister died, but maman loved to give bread away to those who didn't have any at all or very little. Especially to large families who so often went hungry. Good warm bread because the smell stays with you and your clothing for quite some time. It really smells of home, just like the homemade piccalilli. Good warm bread because I still have the memory of it deep down inside of me that warms me up and comforts me. I'm made up of good hot soup: cabbage soup, pea soup, rice and tomato juice soup, and soup made with chicken broth. Soup is oh, so good especially in wintertime. Winter is so very long over here and it's cold, especially after the holidays. Bone chilling cold. I look outside and see the big snow banks. When you get old, you need something warm to thaw you out and prevent you from thinking about being more and more alone in the world. I'm lonely in winter. Some good hot soup warms up the old *canayen*----that's a word that means the old Canadian noggin. I'm made up of cotton, not silk, nor lace. The person that I am is woven of very strong threads, strong enough to last and to hold. I don't tear easily since I last and last like the heavy yellow cotton from the mills, and the beautiful printed calico with nice little flowers that was used for bags of grain. Oh yes, I'm also made up of flowers, especially the wild flowers that don't cost us a dime. God, *l'bon Djieu*, put them there just for us, so that we can appreciate them. All you have to do is look at them, really look at them, because one can so easily miss seeing them. The beautiful colors with petals soft as silk, and the smell of the flowers that caress your nostrils and your heart. I sure am made up of flowers in all of my five senses because I really want to smell the flowers with all my body: touch them, see them, smell them, taste them and even eat them. I want to be caressed by them and let myself be carried away by them beyond my everyday life that sometimes seems so dull. I'm made up of the blue of the sky, because my favorite color is blue. Sky blue, the blue of the Virgin, the blue of the sea, the blue of a bird, the blue of blueberries and the blue that comes to lull my head when I feel blue since I miss my mother, my father, my brothers, my sister, and especially my Willy. I'm made up of prayers, because I say them often. Not that I like to repeat word after word in prayer books, but I like to make up my own prayers, since they come from the heart and not from the mouth. Anyways, God understands what I mean. He doesn't need holy pictures, novenas and loud sighs. I'm made up of words because they're made for us humans. You won't hear animals speaking words. Oh yes, there are some who claim that their sweet pets speak to them, but that's only bragging on their part. I'm made up of words that come from the heart, because they're the best. Words straight from the heart say and mean more than all the others. No lies, no puffed up words, no talking for the sake of talking, just pure words golden and frank like the words of Mémère Tousignant. Mémère Tousignant, what a good person she is! She wouldn't hurt anyone, not even a fly. She has a real heart of gold that one. Never a bad word against anyone; always a good word for you. I'm made up of Mémère Tousignant's words. And I'm made up of dreams. Not daydreaming and things that make the head spin. No. Dreams that bring back the nice memories of the laughter of friends and those that we have loved. Dreams that some day we'll have less sorrow and a bit more love in the world. Dreams of being pretty in the eyes of others who find me ugly, because they don't know that inside, I'm beautiful. I know. Willy knew it. Dreams of belonging because when you're put down by others, that's like a stab to the heart. Dreams that everyone will live in harmony. No fighting nowhere. Dreams that *Messieurs les curés,* the pastors, learn how not to hurt anyone. Dreams that Médée will never leave me. And on top of it all, I'm made up of children, of laughter, kisses and the beautiful clear eyes of children. Children that I never had. Children that I will never have. I know that, from time to time, children give me a hard time, not all, but there's some. They don't do that because they're mean, but it hurts just the same. It's because I love them. They don't stay young too long; they grow up fast. You must take them as they are and love them while they're still young.

I remember one day a little boy came to my door to bring me wild flowers. It was Médée who opened the door and then shouted for me to come and see the boy. I had heard the boy talking. He wasn't much older than ten. He didn't ask to see the *la Souillonne*. Madame Maybelle, he said. That really did my heart good. He seemed shy; he was looking down. But for just a moment, he raised his head and I saw his lovely brown eyes, just like those of my Willy. I fell in love with him right on the spot, the little fellow with the wild flowers. I'm made that way, what else can I say? *Chus, qui chus.* I'm what I am, no more, no less. I think that after God made me, he broke the mold. No more of that, he said. So you see, I'm unique. Not the best, but the only one of a kind. But, some people like me the way I am. My Willy did.

Old Beliefs

Sometimes we have to look back, way back when, and then think about what we inherited from our ancestors. Not always some good things, like the booze and the swear words, but there are some things that are worthwhile keeping. Like the old beliefs, *les vieilles croyances*, as my mother used to say. Isn't it strange how our old folks of years gone by believed in all kinds of things, sometimes in foolish things. Not church beliefs but things that were repeated from generation to generation. I'm not pious enough and I don't know enough about things to make sense out of church beliefs. I leave that to others. But, I know quite a bit about old folks' beliefs. It's because my mother and my aunts loved gabbing together. They would uncover all kinds of things. We also learned a lot from my grandmother Cantin who used to take the family history apart like peeling an onion. She did it with her sister who was called *La Rouge*, the redheaded one and her son Pink's wife, *La Bleue*, the blue one. They all had names of colors in that family. Don't know why. They even had a son who was called *Ti Blanc*, Whitey. I guess that sometimes these ladies didn't know what to talk about, so they talked about beliefs. Like burying the eyes of a potato to make warts disappear. You must not count the stars with your finger because you'll have warts. A shooting star means that there will be a death in the family. A bird that comes to peck at a window means that someone will die. You must not open an umbrella inside a house because that brings bad luck. You must not rock a rocking chair when no one is sitting in it because it brings bad luck or even death. Singing at table means that someone will cry later. Putting your clothes inside out means that it's going to rain. A baby who takes daytime for nighttime and night for day, we make him tumble head over heels. It's supposed to make him sleep when it's time. If you stare at someone in the eye too long, you're going to be cross-eyed. As for mumps, you have to rub the throat with a piece of pig's trough. If you cut your nails on a Sunday, that brings bad luck. If you drop a knife, a fork or a spoon on the floor it will bring company. A man for a knife and a woman for a fork. If your child get the jaundice, well you have to make him pee in a carrot that was hollowed out with a knife, and you tie it on the bedpost. *Le trois fait l'mois*, the third makes the month, is an old saying that people used to say. If it's nice on the third of the month, then it's going to be nice all month long. If it's messy weather, then it's going to be nasty all month long. I don't really know if it always turns out that way. I think this saying was made up by old farmers who relied so much on the weather for their crops. Then there's the belief of hanging your rosary on the clothes line if a girl wants nice weather for her wedding day. You have to hang it out the night before. It stays there all night long. I will always remember when *mémère* Lacourse's Pauline hung her rosary on old lady Tibbetts' clothes line. She was English that one. Her ancestors came from England. She hung it there because Pauline's grandmother didn't have a clothes line on account she had no backyard. On top of it all, Mrs.Tibbetts was Protestant. Pauline thought that her prayers would be answered anyway, like all other brides-to-be. Well, it rained that morning. Did it ever rain. Buckets! All day long. People said that Pauline shouldn't have done what she did. Hang her rosary on old lady Tibbetts' clothes line. Why? Because the Virgin Mary doesn't answer prayers when a rosary is hung on a Protestant's clothes line. Didn't she know that? I'll always remember Pauline's rosary on the wrong clothes line and the rain that fell that day..

There are other things that you learn when you're young. Things that other children learned from other children. Like catching a grasshopper and keeping it in your hand tightly closed and telling it, "Give me some honey or else I'll kill you." After a while, you look inside your hand while the grasshopper jumps out and there's some kind of brown spot in the palm of your hand. It's crazy to do that, but the others show you how to do it, and we all wanted to follow the others. We didn't want to be called fraidy cat. Then there's the idea of putting a yellow flower, like a dandelion, under your chin and rubbing it to know if someone likes butter. If it looks yellow under the chin, well you like butter. Things like that. Silly, at times, but when you're young, anything goes into your silly head.

My grandmother made some kind of holy salve. It was to pull out the bad stuff from a wound, like a splinter or even little pieces of glass under the skin. She made her salve with some kind of rosin, a bit of a blessed candle, some holy oil and other things. Then she would kneel in front of her old black stove and say some prayers, while the mixture slowly boiled. I don't know what those prayers were, but I know that she prayed. Then she would put the salve into small white pots and she sold it for twenty-five cents. She didn't do that to make a profit. She did it for herself, her family and for those people who asked for it.

There's also the belief in the seventh child. The seventh boy in one family. All one after another. No girls in between. Then the seventh son had a gift. The gift of healing. Not his own family, but others. They said that he couldn't heal his own children either nor his wife. It's aunt Eva who told me that because her own father was a seventh child. When he was living in Canada, the bishop, who was going to confirm him, found out that he was a seventh boy child. Well, the bishop took him aside and told him-----his name was Arthur----- that he had a special gift and he asked him to heal his mother who was in a wheel chair. My aunt told me that the old lady started to walk after Arthur had prayed over her. Well, he was a seventh child, after all, and people believed in this. Arthur healed people all of his life. They used to come and talk to his wife, my aunt's mother. Then they would ask her to talk to her husband and have him heal them. Whoever they happened to be. My aunt told me that the children in the household knew when their father was in the process of healing someone because he turned very pale for days on end since it was draining all of his strength. But no one talked about it. Never.

My own father had the gift of healing burns. Those who got burned by fire. He could stop the burning sensation. He had another gift. He could stop someone from bleeding. But that someone had to come and ask him to stop the flow of blood. They usually came to ask my mother to speak to my father for them. That's the way it was done. I've seen it happen. No one talked about that at home. Later on, after my father died, my mother told me all about how it was done. Well, it was a gift handed down from a woman to a man and a man to a woman, and it continued like that. I think that they were special prayers that my father said. He never passed it on to another. Not that I know of. He never passed it on to me. Beliefs like that seem to disappear nowadays. Maybe because people no longer believe in things like that. Well, I'll have you know that those beliefs really worked. You can't always be wary of these things. In the old days people had to believe in something because doctors weren't always available, and people didn't always have the money to pay doctors' fees. In those days, doctors and lawyers, that was for rich people, not for folks like us, and especially not for poor starving people. And so, they had their beliefs. That's all they had, these old folks. And they hung onto them for fear of losing them with time. That's why they handed them f rom one generation to the next. Old beliefs have practically disappeared. People make fun of them and of those who still believe in them. I still believe in many of them because I hold on to whatever links me to the past and my family. I don't want those things to disappear completely even though there are some things that should vanish like old superstitions. I don't believe much in not rocking an empty rocking chair. However, I don't do it. One never knows. And, I don't open an umbrella inside the house simply because it's stupid. That's why.

The Week of Four Thursdays

Now I'm going to talk about something that's a bit curious and at the same time very true. It's the week of four Thursdays. You're going to say, what does that mean, the week of four Thursdays. Let me tell you. It means, never. It's a curious way of saying never, but you know that our ancestors loved to talk, not with big words but with old sayings or phrases they had learned from generation to generation. These things probably came from France with the settlers. You know that Canada was called New France a long time ago. It was at the very beginning of it all. Yes, the settlers, those who came directly from France and got mixed in with the Indians. Well, they brought their ways of saying things that we've kept, like the week of four Thursdays. I'm not very smart but I know things that were said to me either by the family, friends or some acquaintance that I got to know over the years. We don't only learn in school, I'll have you know. We can also learn while listening and watching others. I always had the hankering for learning things. That's why I learn fast. All kinds of things. I don't brag about it, but I'm glad to know these things.

You should know that the week of four Thursdays doesn't stop there. I know that it means never, but never is a word that's sometimes hard to swallow. Then, why four Thursdays? Why Thursday and not the other days of the week? When I think about it, I come up with all kinds of reasons. First of all, I think of how that saying came to be. You have to shake up the noggin sometimes and get at the bottom of things. I don't take everything at face value. Well, when I think about it, it couldn't have been on a Monday because we'd have four wash days in the same week. It couldn't have been Tuesday either because there would have been four ironing days, and it couldn't have been Wednesday, on account there would have been four days of mending. Not Friday either because we would have had four days of not eating meat, and not Saturday either because we would have had to eat beans for four days. Not Sunday, because we would have had to go to mass four times. So, it makes a lot of sense that it's Thursday since, on that day, we can rest and go visit neighbors and do practically anything we want to, and that's why it had to be the week of four Thursdays. That's my way of thinking. It may not make sense to everyone, but it does to me.

When someone tells you that it will absolutely be nice the very day you don't want it to rain-----because you don't want to get all wet that day-----that's in the week of four Thursdays. When someone promises you that he's going to come and fix something and that it won't cost you a cent, well, that's in the week of four Thursdays. When Albertine Bonchamp, Titine, as we call her-----I've known her for years and years-----tells me that she's going to stop putting her nose in people's affairs, well that's in the week of four Thursdays. I just hope that if it has to be, I mean dying, the devil will come and get me in the week of four Thursdays, and I pray that the good Lord will come much before I change my mind on when I leave this earth, because death and me are not very good friends. I'm not scared of dying, I'm scared of being scared.

The week of four Thursdays is not on any calendar. Its not in the doctor's appointment book nor tooth pullers' lists. It's only in the head, and it's only the French-Canadians who understand what it means. The others just don't get it. It's part of our way of saying things. Yes, the week of four Thursdays is well said if you think about it. It forces us to use our noggins. It's much better than using the word, never. Never is such an unkind word. It's so direct and final. Ah! yes, the French-Canadians were not so dumb, I'll have you know. It's not the English who were the brightest of the lot, you know. It's the French-Canadians. They invented all kinds of things even some sayings, and they stuck.

The Back Door

You must know what it means when people say someone has no back door. Well it means that someone has nothing to hide. Very direct, no matter what. Doesn't hide what she's thinking. That she's not a hypocrite and not afraid of telling the whole truth. I like people like that. I don't like people hiding things from me. No back door with me. There are some who always use the back door to say things they don't like saying. They hide behind things. They don't want to hurt anyone, or they want to cover up things. There's even some who want to butter up people just to get favors from them or to get some news about such and such, just to stick their noses in everything. I have no back door. I say what I mean and I mean what I say. It's because I don't want to be accused of being two-faced. I can't stand those who are two-faced. Can you imagine someone telling you something and it takes so long to get to what they want to really say? It's awfully boring and tiring. I know a woman who always takes the back door to say something. She butts in our conversations and winds up twisting the truth. Just like a devilish snake. We never know what she's thinking. Sometimes she gets her words mixed up. She doesn't know what to say and how to say it anymore. It's so aggravating. One day Cora asked her if she knew a certain person who had received a letter from a lawyer because her sister-in-law thought that this person was talking about her when she went to see the neighbors. Well, she told her that she already knew about it. It was a big fat lie because Cora made up the story just to catch her in her lies. Poor

Valéda-----that was her name. I can tell you her name, now that she's dead. She died a year ago.

I know another one, this time a man. He sure didn't use any back door. He went through the front door and massacred the people he talked to in the process. He massacred them with his loud tone of voice and his way of saying things. Just like a bully. He gave it to you, pow! right in the face, not thinking that he was tearing apart the person he was talking about. No common sense with him. He didn't know how to do things. It's good to tell the truth, but sometimes it's better not to say it if it hurts somebody. I mean breaking someone's heart. That's not only dumb but cruel.

Yes, the back door, I wonder who invented that, and was it done just to talk about doors. It's because there are so many ways of saying things with the word, door. I guess our ancestors used to like to talk about doors. Take for example the way of talking about someone's ears and how big they are: to have ears like barn doors. It's because barns have really big doors and at the same time it gives us the idea of how big the ears are. There's also the way of saying that a man's fly is open: his barn door is open. That's what I used to tell little boys who had not zipped up their flies after going to the toilet, "The barn door is wide open". At first, they didn't know what I was talking about, but later on they caught on. Then, they would have a silly grin on their faces.

Then there are all kinds of doors: double doors, *fausses portes*, passageway doors, screen doors, arch doors, the little doors of a stove, cellar doors and barn doors. That's not even mentioning mill doors and church doors. Churches have back doors, not only front doors. But the back doors of a church are smaller. You'll never see a bride going through the back door. Aunt Rosée loved to make us laugh with her different ways of using words. Well, she used to say *porte-crotte*-----that's turd carrier-----are only good for back doors because their behinds are so big that they should hide them. Then she'd talk about the doors of heaven and the doors of hell. There's only one in heaven, she said, because people that are saved all pass through it, while there are many doors in hell, because there are so many who go to hell, and that's why there are many to let everyone go in. I guess aunt Rosée didn't believe that too many people went to heaven. Poor aunt Rosée, she was so scrupulous that lady. She used to say that women couldn't reveal too much of their body. They had to cover the chest up to the neck and even the arms, and no short skirts. Modesty, she called it. Well, some women are so modest that they become scrupulous. Aunt Rosée prayed all day long and said her rosary all in one long stretch, mumbling along as fast as she could. Her lips would move as if she was hurrying all the time. One big, long mumble. But she was a good person, aunt Rosée. No back door with her.

Christ's Stories

Ever since I didn't go back to church on account of *Monsieur le cure* who made me feel ashamed, I started to read the Bible every Sunday. It's because I didn't want to feel like I was a Protestant and that I didn't pray. I wasn't a godless person. I'll have you know that I continued to pray, since I knew that God would understand. He understands much better than the *curés*. We don't need to be in church to pray to God, the Holy Virgin and the saints. Especially those who answer our prayers like Saint Anthony, Sainte Thérèse, the good Sainte Anne and the good Saint Joseph. I have a statue of all of them. Also Brother André of Montreal. He hasn't been declared a saint yet but, for me, he is a saint. I have a holy picture of him. He has such a kind face.

Coming back to my Sunday reading, there are some who told me that a Catholic shouldn't read the Bible. It was forbidden reading. That those who knew what needed to be known in the Church, and who know what Catholics ought to do or not do, for them, an ordinary Catholic like me, reading the Bible was like reading a forbidden book. I never knew that. One never saw Bibles in our homes then. Only at mass when the priest read the gospels. He could do it because he was a priest, a man consecrated by the bishop. Even his fingers were consecrated. That's why a person like me couldn't touch a priest, even though I would have wrung *Monsieur le curé*'s neck when he got all riled up that Sunday. The priest at the retreat had told us about a priest being consecrated, fingers and all, when he was preaching from the pulpit. You had to believe it. Well, after

41

what happened with the *curé*-----it wasn't my fault it was his-----I bought myself a Bible at Fishman's Five and Dime. You know, the big store on Main Street where you can get almost anything for a low price. It was a cheap one, but I knew that God would understand. I couldn't afford one with gold on the edge of the pages and a leather cover with beautiful letters in gold. That was expensive. No wonder us poor workers could not buy one of those. Besides, I thought that God's word was not cheap, even though the little book was cheap. The Bible was in English. I understand English, enough to be able to make things out. I told myself that if it was a holy book that told us about God's revelations, as the priests say, well then what God has told us through those who wrote the Bible can't do us any harm. That if God doesn't want me to read the Bible, well, he'll come and stop me one way or another, like send lightning to split my head in two. It hasn't happened yet, and I continue reading the Bible every Sunday morning while Médée is sleeping.

I love to read Christ's gospels. I mean the stories that he tells others. It's funny but I don't like to say Christ too much, because it sounds like a swear word. I don't like the sound of the word, but that's the way it is. I say it because it's a word from religion. Well, the stories in the Bible that Jesus tells are very interesting. They entertain while making us think. I love those stories. Christ was a good teller of tales just like old man Deschambault. That old man sure could tell stories. Nice stories, not silly ones or dirty ones.

I'm sure that Jesus knew a lot of people who could neither read nor write. Dumb people too. All kinds of people. As for the apostles, they weren't all stars, you know. There were some who weren't the brightest, like Saint Peter. Not that I want to say anything bad about him but sometimes he seems to be just a little bit dumb. In any case, that's how I see things in the Bible. That's why Jesus told stories, and sometimes he had to explain them to the apostles because they didn't understand everything he told them. They were hard-headed. Probably their minds had stayed back there in their fishing nets. As I see it, most of them were poor ignorant people like me. It wasn't their fault, like it's not my fault either. It's nobody's fault. You have to take things as they come. You mustn't get all shook up over it. But, I'm going to tell you that a person, even though she may be dumb, can learn if she wants to. It depends on us. You have to get out of your rut and do something. Not stay there doing nothing and complaining to God all the time. He's got a lot of other things to take care of. Like the starving ones, the very poor, the children who are alone in the world, the women who are abandoned by their husbands and those who get killed at war and many others. He must see things, so many things as high up as he is. Hard things that tear the heart apart. Sometimes I tell myself I would like it if he could arrange things a little better. But what can we mortals do about it. He's the one who fixes things in life. His way, not ours. Our way might not always be best either. I don't know. I know very little about such things. All I know is that I wish things would straighten out in my life. That people would stop not liking me. But I can't complain. The worst thing is that I'm alone. Alone without my Willy. Médée is just a friend who lives with me. I stay out of his way and he stays out of mine. *Comme ça, on s'chicane jamais*, we never fight.

My favorite story, the one I love the most in all of the gospel stories, is the one about the Samaritan woman. She had a kind heart that woman. I don't know why she was scorned by others. It seems that she was off the track, and that the other Jews didn't like her. I don't know why. It probably was part of the politics of the time. I don't much care for politics. Always bad-mouthing each other. The Samaritan woman was only trying to get some water at the well when there was nobody there. She was probably afraid of the Jews, and they probably would have chased her away. Why couldn't they get along these people? Anyways, there were no faucets then. It was like us on the farm. We had to go fetch water outside at the pump. Well, Christ asks her for some water because he must have been thirsty. He had walked a very long time in the dust. So, he starts to talk to her. She saw that he wasn't like the others who had a grudge against her for whatever reason, I guess. The story begins to be interesting when Jesus speaks to her about water that tastes so good that you don't ever get to be thirsty again. I'd want some of that water, if we could get it nowadays. Because, I wouldn't have to drink anymore. But, I would miss my glass of beer, now and then. It's a good thing that this water that kills all thirst once and for all doesn't exist. However, I realized later, while re-reading the story of the Samaritan woman, that Christ probably wanted to say that this water was not water after all but eternal life. Eternal water. Going to heaven with him. He was very smart that Jesus. He knew how to tell a story about water to the Samaritan woman and tell her the truth about herself. Like he knew how many husbands she had gotten. Five. And the man she was living with was not her husband either. I guess she was shacking up. I'm staying with a man, but I'm not shacking up. God knows I'm not.

The other story that I like a lot is about the prodigal son. I didn't know what was meant by "prodigal," so I asked the old maid, Héloïse Pinard, who lives right next door and taught school all her life. She never married, and I don't even know if there was a Willy in her life. Poor Willy, taken away from me when he was still young. I miss him so terribly much! No one will ever know how much. Anyhow, Héloïse told me that it meant a child who leaves home and spends all of his inheritance. In the story, Jesus talks about a father-----no mother----and two boys. The younger one tells his father, "Give me my share of the money," and then leaves. He goes far far away. After spending all his money, he realizes there's a famine in that part of the world. Everyone's starving. The boy begins to go hungry and becomes needy. He finds a job taking care of pigs. He's really at the end of his rope. He was even thinking of eating swill. That's being really hungry. Can you imagine eating swill? He says, here I'm starving and back home the employees eat bread every day. He decides to go back home. At least, there, I'll no longer be hungry with cramps in my stomach, he tells himself. It's not funny at all when someone is that hungry, enough to put a hole in the stomach. And he must have been ashamed of what he had done, but his hunger was bigger than his shame, I guess. I'm telling the story as I understand it.

Well, he starts to walk and walk for months until he finds himself back home on the farm. He really thought that his father would scold him, but his father receives him with open arms. Without bearing a grudge. That's what I call a good father. No bad feelings either. He tells his servants-----I guess he was very rich to have servants----- "Go and fetch a robe for him." They bring the boy a robe and put rings on his fingers. Well, at that time men wore robes, you know. They didn't have pants then. Jesus and Saint Joseph didn't wear pants. I never saw pants in holy pictures, nor in the beautiful holy portraits on the walls. It wasn't like women's dresses, no, it was men's robes. Much like the bathrobes of today, I think. And the father has the fattest calf killed. That's good meat, tender and sweet, I'll have you know, especially the milk calves. Everyone is celebrating except for the brother of the prodigal son. I don't know their names because the story doesn't say. Well, the brother was mad as hell against his father for the simple reason that he had never gone outside the farm, and had worked all of his life and never gotten a feast in his honor. I think that wasn't fair. Anyways, the father is very glad to have his lost child back. He couldn't feel otherwise. It's not because he didn't love the older one. It's because his heart was filled with joy after having found his lost son. He wanted to celebrate. It's hard for a father to lose a child, and I understand why the father did what he did. I would have done the same thing even though I'm not a father.

Christ knew so very well what he was saying in this story, because he knew his own father and if he had gotten lost, his father would have done the same thing as the father of the prodigal son. I'm talking about God the Father, not Saint Joseph. Anyways, St. Joseph wasn't his real father. He adopted him. It was easy to do that in those times since the Blessed Virgin needed a husband and the Holy Child needed a father, but that's another story. That's how I see things in the prodigal son story. You have to forgive in life. Sometimes things don't seem fair, but you have to forgive, not seek revenge. I think that's what the story tells us. God the Father is always ready to forgive is the message of this story from what I get out of it. If I would have had children, I would not have harmed them if they had cast me aside. I would have been hurt, but I wouldn't have sought revenge. I'm not any better than the others, but I'm not any worse either. Anyways, if I had been the father I would have given a feast to the other boy also. Because, I think that would have been fairer and it would have fixed things. It wouldn't have hurt the other one as much. But that's my idea on that.

Another story that I love a lot, but bothers me a bit, is the one about the good shepherd. The one who tends his flock of sheep. Well, it bothers me because sheep are not at all as cute as you think they are. If you ever stayed on a farm with sheep, you'd find that they stink and they're not always very clean. The little ones, well that's different. The lambs, I mean. They're more approachable and they're really like pets. As for the ewes and the rams----as my grandfather called them----they're not very clean with their dirty wool coats, kind of mangy-looking, and when they're soaking wet, they stink. Real smelly stuff. Enough to make you do faces, so strong is the stench. Anyways, it's not me who chose those animals for the story.

Christ, I guess, loved sheep. During his time, there were pastures upon pastures of sheep. These people didn't work in cotton mills. They really struggled in life. Not very good soil either. It was rocky. That's what Mrs. Atkinson says. The soil of Jerusalem was rocky. She says, "I'm not Catholic but I'm Christian." That means she reads the Bible. Anyways, the good shepherd loves all of the sheep and they recognize his voice. He takes good care of them. The one who does sheep herding just to earn some money doesn't really know the sheep. He doesn't even know their names. And then, there are those who climb over fences and don't go through the gate, well they're robbers. It's in the story. I'm not inventing things. I guess that Christ was quite a good shepherd because he understood the life of sheep herders and their sheep. He didn't lose a single one. I know that it's only a story, but Christ told it in order to give us a lesson as a school teacher would.

In another part of the story, I read that Christ said that if and when only one sheep got lost, he would leave the other ninety-nine to go and look for the lost sheep. I would say that's not too wise a thing to do, because he runs the risk of losing the others. They need a shepherd to watch over them, and they shouldn't be left behind. I don't know, I'm not one who ever took care of sheep. I don't know how to do that. I suppose that Christ loved it so much, I mean the lost sheep, that he was risking all in order to find it. That's what happens when you love an animal so much that you take risks. I would say it's the same thing with humans. Well, it proves that Christ loves all of us, especially the stray ones. And, you have to include the scared ones, the lame, those with scabs, the drunkards, the hunchbacked, the puny ones, the crushed ones, the dumb ones, the rag pickers, the *Marie-quat'e-poches*-----that's the sloppy ones like the souillonnes----- the ones cast aside by society and all those who are lost or off the track in the sight of others. Everyone. As far as I'm concerned, he could have taken other kinds of animals like puppies or kittens. They're much more lovable. Cleaner too. No goats. They're too stubborn.

I don't want to bore you with Bible stories but here's one more to show you how Christ knew how to tell stories. Stories that tell us something and go straight to the heart. The story of the good Samaritan is the story about a poor man who's in the ditch and who was beaten and kicked in the face, and left there by robbers. A priest arrives on the scene and goes right by. I guess he didn't want to bother with him. He didn't want to get dirty, or he was afraid of catching something. Then a Levite comes along. I don't know what a Levite is. It's probably a Protestant who comes from far away. He steps on the other side, not to come face to face with the man in the ditch. Comes a Samaritan and he takes good care of the poor man. Christ often talks about Samaritans, just like the woman at the well who wants water. They must have been good people, those Samaritans. Well, Jesus talks about them and doesn't call them hypocrites. Never. I don't like hypocrites and those who show off like the Pharisees. They're a bunch of wise guys. I can't stand them. It was the Samaritan who was merciful towards the man in the ditch, as the story says. That's why I often hear people say of someone, he's a good Samaritan. Now I get it. I like to help people out when I can do some good, and that's good for the heart. I guess I'm a good Samaritan too.

The one I don't understand too much is the story of Jonas in the whale, and when Christ talks about the sign of Jonas. That, I don't understand. He's speaking too much in riddles, as far as I'm concerned. And all those things he uses in his story, like the queen who's coming at noon and something about salmon, that's all beyond me. Well the apostles used to catch lots of fish. They earned their living with that. So salmon makes sense to me. All I know about Jonas is what the nuns taught me. They said that Jonas had lost his balance when he was in his boat. He fell in the water and he practically drowned. A huge whale swallowed him, and he stayed there for three days. It must have smelled like rotten fish inside there. Anyways, the whale threw up and spit him out. Well, like anyone who throws up his supper. But, I'm telling you, I don't understand the sign of Jonas at all. I understand the story, but not the sign. I'd have to ask *Monsieur le curé* but he's mad at me. I think I'll ask mémère Archambault. She knows a lot of things and she reads cards. She must know something about signs.

The last thing that I want to say about Christ's stories-----because I don't want to bore you with all of that-----it's when Jesus says that the poor are blessed, and especially when he says that if you give a banquet, don't invite the rich, not even your friends, but the poor and the lame. That's being really generous. How many would do that? I never was invited to a banquet. I'd love that, but I don't know anyone who would invite me because I'm poor and they call me the Souillonne. It's not a sin being poor, but sometimes it's inconvenient. What can I say? Besides Médée, I'm all alone like a lonely dog. A little dog who would be satisfied with the crumbs off the table, like poor Lazarus. Not to complain, but I'd love it so if someone would only come and visit me from time to time. Sometimes, I'm fed up seeing Médée and his bottle of Ballantine. Well, that's why, at times, I ask him for a glass of beer.

Washing and Cleaning

Washing and doing regular housework, that was every week, but the *grands ménages,* as my mother said-----that's spring cleaning-----that was a lot of work, and with us French-Canadians it was both spring cleaning and fall cleaning. Weeks of work. That's the fault of women. They never stop cleaning, scraping and rubbing, and they do it so very well. Not the men, though. If it weren't for the women, it would never get done. I mean the spring and fall cleanings. Men would live in dirt. When a woman puts her hand to it, then things move fast, I guarantee you. We women, why we're dirt busters, rubbing and scraping experts, cleaners, floor washers, wall washers and doers of windows and cupboards. We wash everything that needs to be washed with soap and water. One thing we're not, we're not sloppy cleaners. We don't do messed up jobs. When a person half washes a wall or the floors, well that's slipshod work, a mess. Weekly washing of clothes, well that's another thing. You have to wash with care because our clothes would turn yellow and it would smell bad after a while. Washing the clothes starts early Monday morning and it lasts until late afternoon, and sometimes up to evening. It depends on the clothes line and, of course, the weather.

My mother would get up at quarter to five on Monday morning to start her wash. She had her boiler already filled with water, one pail at a time, right there on the kerosene stove. She lit her burners and separated her clothes, the whites, the colors and my father's overalls as well as her sons', when they were living at home. It's because overalls were work clothes, especially my father's overalls since they were full of oil and grease, on account he was a loom fixer. My father and one of my brothers worked in the mills. The other brother worked in a shoe shop. My sister and me, well, we were too young to go to work. We went to school. My sister died young. Flora was her name. She was only fifteen. She died of scarlet fever. She had to stay in bed by herself in a separate room, and only my mother could take care of her. She would put on long rubber gloves and she'd go in her room five or six times a day. The doctor wanted my sister to go to the hospital, but my mother and my father refused. They wanted to take care of her themselves. Anyways, my sister died at home. There wasn't any showing of the body and they buried her the same afternoon that she died. My mother and my father would have liked to have at least a *libera* at church, but the doctor and the others said that we had to bury her as soon as possible. Poor her, buried like a dog.

Let's get back to the washing. Once the clothes are sorted, my mother checked the water to make sure it was hot enough, then she would transfer the hot water to her washing machine. If the water was too hot-----after all it was boiling water-----she would then put in some cold water just to cool off the hot water a bit, because we don't put clothes in boiling water, since it would take hold of the dirt and the dirt would remain in the clothes a very long time. Then she would put some boiling water in another tub and add bleach. That was for sheets, pillow cases and the men's white shirts. In yet another tub, she'd put cold water with bluing. That was to make the wash smile with cleanliness, she said. Then she would wring everything in her wringer, except for things she didn't want to be wrinkled too much. That, she wrung by hand. Then after three or four washes, she'd do the overalls with some slivers from a big bar of yellow soap added to the hot water. That was beside the washing powder like Rinso Blue or Oxydol. It depended on a sale at Audie's market, if there was one. But with overalls, my mother was a scrubber. She scrubbed and she scrubbed until her knuckles turned red. Well, she didn't want people saying that she didn't know how to clean and wash clothes. The stains didn't always go away, but at least she had done her best.

If it was nice outside, my mother hung her wash on clothes lines, because clothes smell so good when hung outside. She had two nice long clothes line that went from both corners of the window frame up to the tree in the back yard. She loved her clothes lines and her pulleys. There's nothing like drying your clothes outdoors, she used to say. It smells so fresh. Especially the bed sheets. When you jump into bed, you feel the freshness all over your body and everything smells so nice and so fresh. And when you hang outdoors, it shows the neighbors that you know how to wash. The old lady Demeule didn't know how to wash clothes. Well, she wasn't a French-Canadian; she had married one, but she herself wasn't French. Her name was Frances Demeule; people called her, Franny. Apparently she hadn't learned from her mother. Her wash was always gray, especially her sheets and pillow cases. We could see that she had only half washed her clothes. "I'd be ashamed to put that outdoors where everyone can see," my mother used to say. "We're not rich but we're clean."

My mother had to empty her washing machine by the pailfuls, then her two tubs, dry everything, even her boiler, and put things back into place. It took her at least half of the afternoon. Sometimes, I helped her when I came home from school. She was dead tired, but she didn't complain. Never. Then it was time for supper. I peeled the potatoes. She used to say to me before I started peeling, go do your homework. That was more important. Sometimes I'd tell her I didn't have any. I didn't like homework at all, you see. But my mother was wise, wiser than me. She knew that the nuns always gave homework. Then I would do it kind of backwards. I didn't dare displease my mother. "You're not going to be a scrubber all your life like me," she used to tell me."You have to do something with your life. That takes education." Oh, I didn't like school. I left school when I was fourteen to help out at home. On account my father had gotten hurt in the mill and he did not go back to work because they didn't want him anymore. No more wages for my father. It tore his heart out. Then my brother lost his job at the mill and he took off, in order to find work somewhere else. He didn't want to stay where there were no jobs. My other brother worked in a shoe shop. He earned very little money.

Anyways, he died not too long after my father fell ill. So, it was me, my mother and my father. We struggled the best we could. I was the only one working in the mill; I was fourteen and a half. I joined the other fourteen and fifteen year olds who worked in the mills. I knew one who started working at thirteen. She was tall for her age and they didn't check papers then. That was all right. We all needed to work and help out. I did my very best. That's about the time my father started to become a drunk, but my mother never called him that. It wasn't his fault, my mother said. He often got discouraged, my father. Sometimes I heard him cry in hiding. We ate baloney, bread with jam, bread with bacon fat, bread with molasses, and even bread with mashed beans. Bread with all kinds of things on it. I didn't mind it as long as we stayed together, my father, my mother and me.

When it comes to cleaning----not the weekly cleaning, but the *grands ménages* of spring and fall----I'm telling you things did not cool down. My mother went about her work like a bat out of hell. The worse thing was that she dragged me in it. At the beginning, I didn't like it too much but, with time, I learned how to tolerate it. I had to since my mother was alone to do all of that work plus the meals. That's besides doing the weekly wash. My mother worked ever so hard in her lifetime. Poor thing, never a nasty word. She always had a smile on her lips. With chapped hands and her feet dead tired, she would rub her back and sometimes let go long sighs. I just looked at her and I found her to be so good, my mother.

It wasn't enough washing all of the dishes that we used during the week, we had to wash those we never used. After all it was *le grand ménage.* Like all the glasses on the top shelf, way up high in the cupboard. "Why do you keep all of those glasses?" I used to ask her every big cleaning. "Because they're wedding gifts," she would tell me. "But they're not dirty." "You don't see the dust that gathers there up top; we have to wash them so that they'll shine like new. We don't skip over things just because we don't use them." She sang that same refrain to me each time we did the big cleanings. Well, I stopped asking her questions about her *grands ménages* because she'd always answer me the same way, "You don't understand, that's all." Wash the glasses, wash the bowls, wash the plates, wash the candy dishes that we never used except on New Year's Day, wash and dry the punch bowl with its eight little cups, then put the bowl and the cups in a big cotton sack that my grandmother had made. She took good care of that punch bowl as if it were the apple of her eye. Why? Because it had belonged to my great-grandmother. It was precious like gold and silver. What I didn't understand at all was the fact that my mother never used that punch bowl. She didn't even drink. Anyways, I gave it away to my friend, the Irish woman, Bessie, who had broken hers. She had a big family and she served eggnog at Christmas. I'm so glad that my friend uses it because I like pleasing her. What would my mother do with a punch bowl in her grave? It's so true, that we bring nothing with us when we're dead. I have nothing. So, I'll have no baggage to bring along when I kick the bucket.

Once the cleaning was done, my mother sat in her rocking chair and had a big smile on her face. Her eyes sparkled. Her *grand ménage* was done. One more time. "Thank God for giving me the strength to carry on one more time," she would say. After she got sick and couldn't do any more cleaning, I'm the one who did it. Sometimes she used to check on me to see if I was doing it right. I have to admit that, at times, I made round corners and didn't do everything exactly the way my mother did. As for the darned glasses, I did some here and there, but not all of them. She didn't even notice. She was happy as if I had done them all. That's to show you how a person can be so attached to her cleaning and scrubbing all her life. She was cleaner than clean, my mother. She was scrupulous in her *ménage*. Just for the pride of being clean. Just to have a sense of things sparkling clean, even though it was hidden on the top shelves of the cupboard. I'm not as clean as my mother was, but I'm not dirty either. I'm not the *souillonne* people make me out to be. Not at all. La Souillonne is clean. She washes and she cleans. She's not the filthy one that people make her out to be. No 'mam!

The Funny Stuff

Isn't it funny when you hear people talk sometimes. At times, they talk as strange as they walk. That's how people say it. To talk as strange as they walk. It means, if someone walks bad, well they talk bad. Not the lame or the crippled. Those who have a hard time walking. No. I mean those who are not careful when they speak. Like mister Létendre. They say that he often talks through his hat, even though he doesn't wear one. I know that it means that he talks without knowing what he's talking about. Funny stuff like that. But what's really funny is the way that things turn out sometimes. Like smoking. It's all right for men and young guys to smoke; it's a sign of being a man. Hey! Smoking the cigarette or the pipe is a mark of having arrived into manliness. Smoking a cigar means he's a man of distinction. High class. We all know that young people often smoke in hiding, girls and boys alike. I know, I tried it myself once and it stuck in my throat, and I started coughing and coughing. I smoked that weird stuff, corn hair. You know, the yellow stuff that's at the top of a corn husk. I don't know how they call that but we called it, corn hair, *des ch' feux d'blé d'Inde*. We used to roll it in strips of newspaper. And did it stink. Things that young people weren't supposed to do and they did it anyways. I did it just once with Ti Paul St. Michel. He had dared me to smoke. Just to see if I would do it. Then Ti Paul told on me. He told my mother and my father spanked me with a strap. I never did it again. Coming back to our tale about smoking, men smoke and that's acceptable. They can smoke anywhere. But, it's not allowed for women. We say that their reputation is in danger when they smoke, and those that do smoke well, they're called good-for-nothings. Their reputation. What does that mean, their reputation? I know it means how others think of them. But, how about the reputation of men? Anyways, it's funny stuff. Don't make me believe that's it's not.

Now I want to talk about Thanksgiving. It's supposed to be a holiday to thank the good Lord. Thank him for the year with its harvest and the good things that he gave us. First of all, most people don't even know what we mean by harvest. They were never farmers and worse than that, they never lived on a farm and knew nothing about it. Harvest doesn't mean much to them. They buy all their stuff at the grocery store. But the stores charge them for what they buy, and stores make a darn good profit. Why tell them thank you? Thank you for what? For letting them make a profit? And moreover, Thanksgiving is a holiday for the English. They're the ones who started it. It started on a rock in Massachusetts. They say that a boat from England came and landed there many years ago. They met the Indians who ate almost nothing but corn. They got together, the English and the Indians, and they made supper with what they had. I suppose they thanked God each in their own way. As for the Indians, there was someone called the manitou. That manitou lived in the trees and in the air. Well, it's Aurore Bellefeuille who put that in my head because there's mixed blood in her family. Her great great grandfather had married a pure Indian in Canada, when the whites mixed in with the Indians. What's funny about Thanksgiving is the idea of eating turkey. I would have preferred instead a good stuffed pork shoulder like *mémère* used to make. And then, all of those candles in the shape of a turkey, corn and pumpkins. And all their pumpkin pies. We didn't make pumpkin pies at home, we made molasses pie, blueberry pies, sugar pies or raisin pies. Those were pies, yes 'mam! Thanksgiving, that doesn't come from us French-Canadians. It comes from the English who wanted a day off, not that it's a bad idea at all. Funny stuff as far as I'm concerned.

Arthémise Tranchemontagne-----now that's a name for sleeping outdoors as we say it-----had the same first name as his father. I guess you would say he was a junior. Well, that's what people say. He was proud to say that his father made root beer in his bathtub. Not everybody had a bathtub then. He wanted to keep his bathtub just for the making of root beer. His wife fought with him over the bathtub because she wanted him to let her use it for baths for herself and the kids. The father didn't take baths. Oh, he used to wash, from time to time, when his wife got after him, but he never set foot in a bathtub. He washed at the kitchen sink. His wife got mad one day and she lifted her little husband in her arms-----he only weighed ninety-eight pounds and measured four feet ten-----and she threw him in the bathtub while he was making his root beer. Arthémise's wife was a big woman who weighed at least two hundred and forty pounds, and she was strong, as strong as a horse. She took her little husband in hand, I tell you. He was smeared with root beer, he was, and he smelled of root beer. That's why he had to take a bath in the tub. He took a liking to it, I guess, because he took a bath every week after that. Besides, his wife had told him that she wouldn't sleep with him if he didn't take a bath in the bathtub every week. He never made any root beer after that. He bought it at the store. Yes, that's another one for the funny stuff, the story of the little husband and the root beer bathtub.

Don't' you find it strange when someone tells you a funny story and it's not funny at all? My cousin, Isabelle, loved to tell stories, but the way she told them, they fell flat like a heavy pancake. She liked to repeat stories she had heard from others, but she didn't know how to tell them. She tried to present herself as a storyteller. She put on airs, Isabelle did. She loved to put on airs. She would have been a not-so-bad actress. Even though a person tells us something funny and it's done wrong, it changes things around and it's not funny. It becomes strange. No one laughs at what is being said, only at the person saying it. Like the time Isabelle wanted to tell *pepère* Cordeau's story. *Pepère* Cordeau knew how to tell a story and make us laugh. Laugh until you had tears coming down your face. Our sides hurt from laughing so much. He told the story of a village *curé* who made his parish rounds and came to this house where a lady, he didn't know too well, lived. She didn't come to church too often but she was a parishioner who gave money to the church when they collected for heating. Well, the story goes, she asked the priest if he wanted some tea. He told her, yes, just to be polite. So, she poured some tea and asked him if he wanted some sugar. He said, yes. She took out some sugar packets from her bodice and gave him a couple. Then she asked him if he wanted some milk for his tea. The good old *curé* became all flustered and did not take any time at all to tell her, "No, no, no." Ha, ha, ha! It's was so funny the way *pepère* Cordeau acted out the story. But, Isabelle told the story upside down because she doesn't like to talk about indelicate things. Indelicate, my eye! All women have bodices and breasts. Some say tits but I don't want to go that far. Anyways, Isabelle told the story that *pepère* Cordeau had said, but instead of the woman taking out sugar from her bodice, she said she took it from her sleeve. It loses all real meaning that way. It's not funny at all. *Pepère* Cordeau's story is not a dirty story. It's very funny if you understand where he's going with it. You don't need any explanation. Perhaps the children might, when they ask what it means, but we tell them that they'll understand later on when they grow up, and go to bed.

Isn't it funny also when someone trips over his own two feet and worse, over his own words. Still worse, over what he does. The lawyer, Laferrière, had a swelled head. He put on airs even though he wasn't any better than the others. He came from the low class end of town and his parents were as poor as ours. But the Laferrières loved to pretend to live on the high branch of their low class. They loved to boast about their boy. Excuse me, no, their offspring, they said. He went to college to learn to be a lawyer and that's thanks to his uncle in Montreal who pushed him some money. Lawyer Laferrière was always dressed up just so. He had a black felt hat on his head, he wore a starched white shirt, a suit that was well pressed and shoes well shined. He wore gloves even in the summertime. One day, our good lawyer went to Madame Desrosiers's house for business. She wanted him to take off his shoes because it was springtime and there was a lot of wet sand in the streets, and even on the sidewalks. She always made her husband take off his shoes when he came into the house, because Madame Desrosiers was super clean. So clean that she cleaned the hands of all her clocks with a toothpick. She didn't want her husband to smoke inside either. It was <u>her</u> house. She sent him down the cellar. Well, lawyer Laferrière didn't want to take off his shoes and he told Madame Desrosiers that he would stay on the kitchen carpet. She told him, no. "Come and sit down in the living room to talk about very important things. Lawyer things," she said. He realized that he had to take off his shoes because he didn't want to lose her business. He takes off his shoes and to Madame Desrosiers' great surprise, the lawyer had big holes in his socks, on the heels and toes. I guess that his mother didn't mend his socks. Madame Desrosiers saw that and started to choke with laughter, but she put her hand on her mouth so as not show her embarrassment too much. Why, she almost laughed out loud right in front of him. The lawyer pretended as if nothing happened and he continued his lawyer business, and then he left. People say that Madame Desrosiers was so ashamed for him that she changed lawyer. That's so funny. I'm not making that up. Démerise Lavertu told me that story. I could tell you some more funny stuff without stopping, but that's enough for now.

Spruce Gum and Things in Nature

Do you know anything about spruce gum? Well, spruce trees grow in the woods. They're like evergreens, or maybe a bit like pine trees. Those trees produce some kind of gum. But, we don't chew evergreen gum or pine gum. It's poisonous. Only spruce gum. My father used to make some spruce gum. I mean he went into the woods to get some. He'd fix it so you could chew it afterwards. I never liked the taste too much; I preferred Spearmint gum when someone gave me some. Mérilda Floribert had some, at times, because her grandmother often gave her a nickel to buy some. She would open the packet and would give me a stick of gum. She bought the one with the white wrapper. There were five sticks in the packet. We used to chew on that until it started tasting like rubber. It had lost all its taste. We threw the gum away after that, but you had to roll it in its foil paper before throwing it away. Not like the guys who used to stick the chewed gum under the school benches we sat on. The nun was wise. If she caught one doing it, she made them stick it on the end of their noses in front of all the class. Can you imagine, a big wad of gum stuck on the nose, with a very red face. Some cried at times. Big babies, the others called them, but I never found that too funny. I would not have liked to be humiliated in front of the class.

There are also many things in nature that we don't know about. I got to know some when I lived on the farm in Canada. I was young then, but I was quite sharp, and I would ask questions to my father.

He would always find time to answer me. As for my grandfather, he'd go after herbs in the woods. He knew about all kinds of them. Why, he knew all their names, like the plantain for whooping cough, *mille-feuilles* for digestion, wild pansies for children's skin problems, a kind of thistle for ulcers and their roots are good for hair loss. Not the sumac nor the lilies of the valley because they're poisonous. Like the rhubarb leaves. You can eat the rhubarb, but not the leaves. It's deadly. It can kill you on the spot. But dandelions are good for the kidneys. I loved it when the yellow flowers turned to white balls of seeds, and I would take a whole handful and I'd blow on them. The seeds would fly everywhere like dust balls in the wind. Little parachutes flying away. Oh yes, my grandfather, he really knew about things in nature and he never went to school. Imagine that!

Nature teaches us many things. I'm talking now not only about nature like the plants, the leaves and the woods but the animals too. All of nature was created by God. There's a reason for all things, my grandmother used to tell me. However, I wonder sometimes-----and I'm talking about animals now-----how Noah got to put all of the animals in his ark. He needed to have two of each, if you remember your bible well: two elephants, two giraffes, two huge crocodiles----I don't like crocodiles for they give me the creepies----two pigs, two horses, two cows----I'm sure the other one was a bull not a cow---- and all that. It must have been a heck of an ark to be able to keep all those animals inside. It must have smelled bad after a week, never mind forty days. I wonder if the flood destroyed everything on earth. Did Noah think of keeping some plants, trees and all that grows, I wonder. He must have brought some seeds of each kind with him because seeds take very little room. It makes perfectly good sense to me. Sometimes, I wonder if Noah really existed. If the flood happened. It must have because it's in the Bible and the Bible doesn't tell lies.

Did you know that late in the fall when the hairs on a caterpillar are well furnished and the fur of a squirrel is thick, it means that winter will come early, and it will be a hard one. When the leaves flip over when the wind starts to blow, it means that it's going to rain.

When the moon takes on the shape of a crescent, it's going to be cold. Or when the moon is hazy and there's a circle around it, the weather's going to turn bad. When rheumatism starts to hurt, it means bad weather's coming. When the sun sets and it's very red, well, it's going to be nice the following day. My mother used to say when the flies start to buzz around your head, it's haying time. *Mémère* Bissonnette used to tell us that when a bird flies very close to a window and touches the pane with its beak, that means someone in the family is going to die. You must never plant a garden before the full moon at the end of May. You're taking a chance that the seeds and the young plants will freeze. Besides, nothing grows too much before the full moon, because the moon attracts the warmth of springtime. That's what the old folks used to tell us. The elderly of the good old days. Yes, the good old times. They weren't always as good as that. Sometimes people went through some tough times. Especially if the land was not too giving of its fruit a given year. Yes, all kinds of signs in nature. Don't believe that all we know comes from school. We can learn a lot of things from the old folks who never sat on a school bench, but have a head on their shoulders. French-Canadians are not dumb. Not at all. Oh, they may be a bit too hardheaded, at times, but they're not dumb. I have to admit there are some who are thick in the head, *des épa's*, as we call them, but they're few and far apart. I'm not thick in the head; I'm just stubborn at times. My mother used to tell me that, and I believed her. She would call me *têtue*. You must surely know that stubbornness is not a fault. It's a sign of will power. That's what I say. Besides, the word *têtu* comes the word *tête* meaning head, and if you're *têtu* then you have a head on your shoulders. That's the way I see it. Not bad for an old *coqu'relle de la Pepperell* as we were called then. That's a cockroach, but you can't make it rhyme in English. You'd have to say, Cockroach of the Pepperell, and that surely doesn't rhyme at all. So much for French into English.

The Button Can

My mother had a button can that she kept on the second shelf of the large cupboard. It was a black can with gold letters and a red spot on top of either side. "Freshly Roasted BOKAR Ground to order COFFEE, A & P Coffee Service," was marked on both sides of the can. I still have that can. I will never throw it away. Well, it's part of my inheritance, along with the old furniture and the dishes that my mother left me. But, the button can, that's precious to me, like gold would be to someone else. All of my life is in there. You're going to say that I'm nuts, but let me tell you why my button can is important to me.

When I was a little girl, I loved playing with my mother's button can. She had kept all those buttons for many many years. She never threw anything away, my mother, especially buttons: buttons from dresses, shirt buttons, coat buttons, all kinds of buttons. Only if she needed special buttons or matching ones for a dress or a coat that she was making did, she go out and buy some on cards at Woolworth's. The button can was the family treasure. We took some to play parchesi. We said, *jouer à vache* but it can't be said like that in English, "play cow"? It wouldn't make sense. It only makes sense in French. I also used to take some to play with my dolls, sometimes. I just loved to empty the can and count the buttons, or look at the special buttons in my hand: plastic pink buttons made like a little flower, red rounded buttons with little flowers all around, shiny metal buttons with a design on top, buttons that looked like pearls and black buttons without holes but with a eye on the back like cassock buttons. Buttons with two holes, four holes and with no holes at all. I've seen some with three holes. White buttons, red buttons, yellow buttons, brown buttons, black buttons, pink ones, blue ones, grays ones, orange ones, green ones and a few moiré buttons. There's an entire world in there.

The button can makes me think of the world because there's all kinds in there. Small ones, big ones, white ones like us, and colored ones like the negroes, the Indians and the Chinese. The world is a whole mixture of people. Just like the button can. There are some that match and others that don't match at all. That doesn't mean they're not good. There's a whole variety in there. Matching is not the real value of the buttons in the button can. Just like people in the world. If an Indian marries a Chinese, well it would be a little funny because we're not used to that. It would be like putting yellow buttons and some red buttons on the same dress. But buttons are buttons, not the world, certainly not people. Things don't have to match all the time because a day will come when everyone in the world will spread out, and we're going to accept marriages with all kinds of people. Like, one day, it will no longer be prohibited to marry a person who's not French-Canadian and not of our religion. Not now, but later. People are not ready yet to mix the different kinds. They don't have the spirit of buttons yet. A day will come also when mothers will no longer keep buttons. They're all going to buy them in stores. We'll throw out the old and we'll only want the new. I'm keeping my button can. It's my little treasure, my little pleasure. From time to time, I take my button can out, I put it in my lap and I empty it in my apron just to look at the buttons and caress them a little with my fingers. Sometimes, tears come to my eyes. That's the way I'm made. On those occasions, I guess I'm the button lady, not that I ever call myself a lady. *La Souillonne aux boutons.* How's that? The buttons' Souillonne.

My Thoughts on That

Well I'm getting there, I mean the end of my stories. I'm telling these stories just to have some fun talking and at the same time share them with those who like to listen to *la Souillonne*. I must admit that I'm beginning to feel my little aches and pains, now and then. You know, those that come with age. My rheumatism bothers me and my feet hurt a lot. Both of my feet are twisted like an old lady who's about to fall apart. Sometimes, it hurts so much that it affects my back. I must have gotten that at the mill when I worked standing up all day long. Forty-three years in the mill running looms. That's besides what I did the years before that. Battery hand and a lot of running around. Good Lord, tell me about tired feet. I had them from morning 'til night. I'm a strong woman, but I'm not made of steel. I too will come to the end of my life some day. My life story. The end. Yes, the final days, *les fins finales* as those who preached the parish retreats used to say. They scared us with that. They didn't stop shouting at us about end of life. Not shouting like shouting out loud at someone, but raising the voice so loud that it scared you. Yes, the end of life when we'll all be judged. I took some and I left some. You can't let it get to you, especially when you have a clear conscience. I'm not ashamed. I did nothing wrong and I don't have it in for no one. Yes, I have a clear conscience. Clear like water from a rock. At least, that's what people say about clear water.

In any case, the Souillonne is not a sloppy one, she's not dumb, she's not without a heart, she not going mad and she doesn't like to say everything she knows out loud, she loves to open up her heart and have a bit of fun. The Souillonne wears underpants, I'll have you know. I'm not an old bag nor a fat sow, and there's nothing wrong with my noggin. I know I'm a bit awkward at times, and I hide myself only when people stare or look at me sideways when I'm outside. That hurts me deep inside. We're not all alike. There are some people who think themselves just so, others who are right in the middle and still others who are completely off the track. I fall between the last two. Someone told me once that I was marginalized. Yes, m-a-r-g-i-n-a-l-i-z-e-d. I answered, "What?" "Well, you're a bit off track, you're not like the others. You don't do like the others do. You act differently than others. And, you belong nowhere. To nobody. You live in the margin of things." All I could think of was the margin of a copybook. The nun used to tell us all the time not to write in the margins. I didn't know I was living in the margin. It must be a place that's not allowed for regular people and especially the irregular ones like me. A place where people want to put me because I'm in the border of things, they insist. I don't give a damn about the margin. I live where I live. I belong there. No one is going to come and tell me where I must stay. All my life, I let people tell me what to do, how to do it and when. By bosses, those who act like bosses, the nuns, the priests, the other children, the guys and even the family. My mother and my father used to tell me what and how to do things, but they told me because they loved me. It was to help me, they said. They didn't do it to boss me around. My Willy never told me what to do and how. He loved me so much, my Willy, enough so as to understand me, Maybelle. There's a way to tell someone something. You mustn't jump on someone and start to blast them with rough language. You have to speak softly and make yourself understood. Any person, even the Souillonne, is not as stupid as that when you begin to understand her. I'm not a button to be thrown in the dump. I'm a button that we keep because I'm worth something, me, Maybelle Sansoucis. I'm not always the Souillonne, I'll have you know. They can call me what they want, but I know who I am. Deep inside of me, I know and feel who I am, and I'm proud of it. That, for certain, I know, but it's hard to make other people understand. Médée knows. *Mémère* Desautels, the old woman who lived upstairs from me-----she's dead now----- she knew. Then there's, the little boy who came to bring me flowers, he knew. Ah, that really warmed my heart. I'm the Souillonne, I'm made that way. I know, I'll never change. I'm like the years that last and last and last. Tomorrow, I'm going to see the doctor. From time to time, my back hurts and my legs feel like rags. It seems to get worse nowadays. It must be because I'm getting old from one end to another. At least that's how we say it in French, *d'un boute à l'autre.* That means it hurts all over. Old mill hands like me learn to live with their hurts and pains. After all, I earned them. Tomorrow, I'll go see the doctor. Just for a short visit. After all, I don't have money to throw away. I can live with my rheumatism. I'm tough to pain. All millworkers are. We're indestructible, I guess. We don't give in to pain and hard times…and we last until the good Lord calls us to himself. I'm not afraid of dying, just the way I'm going to go. I do hope I don't give anyone too much of a hard time, what with taking care of me. You see I have no one. No family left. I'm all alone in the world. I pray to God that he comes and gets me quick. Just like a bug that we slap, and boom! It's gone. Except, I'm not a bug. I'm Maybelle Sansoucis. *La tannante,* the one who makes others laugh with her stories…and sometimes they cry. It's not an ugly name; it's rather a nice name since people who call me that smile as they say it. Here she comes again with her stories that go right to the reality of things. Yes, I'm the one who reminds them of their human side, 'cause I'm no angel. No one is. Only those who try to be one and fail. They fail because of what Héloïse Pinard, the school teacher, once told me: *Qui fait l'ange, fait la bête.*" I said "What?" And she said that it was taken from the thoughts of someone called Pascal----I don't remember his last name. She explained to me that it meant those who try too hard to act like angels, well, they fail. They act foolish instead. If you try to show off your goodness as if you're a goodie-two-shoes, well then you turn into some kind of a monster. You're not natural. Angels are only in heaven and we're not there yet. I know I'm not. I'm right here on this good old earth with my two feet on the ground. I am who I am. I may be *la Souillonne* but I'm first of all, Maybelle Sansoucis. You have to take me the way I am. That's all. 'Til next time. I'll have some others stories to tell you. Oh, do I have some juicy ones for you!

www.ingramcontent.com/pod-product-compliance
Lightning Source LLC
Chambersburg PA
CBHW062020190726

48284CB00012B/1287